FREEDOM'S MAZE

Para Marcela.
Como todo.
Como siempre.

Books by Arturo von Vacano

«Hombre Masa»
«Memoria del Vacío»
«Biting Silence»
«Morder el Silencio»
«Los Laberintos de la Libertad»
 «El Apocalipsis de Antón»
«Sombra de Exilio»

..

FREEDOM'S MAZE

"LIBERATION FROM BRUTE FORCE AND LIES, NO MATTER WHAT FORM THEY TAKE"
ANTON CHEKHOV

Arturo von Vacano

CHARACTERS

ENRIQUE
AND 219 VOICES

Note for the Producer:
Enrique is a middle-class Bolivian.
Once you see one, you have seen them all.

You need to have seen each of the Voices.
If you have, you know them.
If you have not, go and look.
If you look well, your audience will know them.

Excuse our broken English.

All characters but ENRIQUE — and, perhaps, KIKO — are represented by VOICES and
their respective IMAGES. Such VOICES may be illustrated by actors, photos, paintings,
slides or any other conceivable visual means, in accordance with the material possibilities
assigned to each performance.
The text spoken by the Women of Caracoles in MASSACRE is a literal copy of a letter
sent to the U.S. Catholic Church by the women of the Caracoles Mining Center in
Bolivia after the 1980 military coup.

Synopsis of Scenes
South: La Paz, Bolivia
North: New York City
1980

NOTES FOR AN IMPROBABLE PERFORMANCE

FREEDOM'S MAZE attempts to offer a fast glance of ENRIQUE, his past and his background through images of contemporary and historical "types." which may be just pictures or slides.

These pictures should be based on paintings and portraits to be found in books and museums and on photos of anonymous people from newspapers, magazines and their files.

These images should be used with freedom and imagination to articulate an "intimate" reality for each Voice. All Voices must be "built" while they talk. Images and music should struggle for authenticity to convey a deep feeling of the identity of people and places.

Short notes appear next to a few Voices. The Alphabetical Notice on these Voices could be printed with the program of a performance given on a stage made of several slide screens and a central space with a table and a typewriter.

South

(Aymara music. Typewriter typing. Penumbra.)

(A chair and a table. On the table, a typewriter.

Enrique, seated front row center.

Sounds of a crowd in a big hall. Words and sentences in English and Spanish.

A loudspeaker: "Martinez, Pedro. Pedro Martinez. Martinez, Pedro."

Other names. Silence.

Enrique stands up and walks to the table, looking at his shoes. He walks fast.

He sits in front of the typewriter, as if to speak with the Authority.)

Enrique - Here I am. 42. White. Not white? Hispanic? Bueno, Hispanic.
Spanish. Yes. English, no. French, no. Married. Once only, of course. Four
children. A girl, a boy, a girl, a boy. 10, 9, 8, 29. (Lights a cigarette.) I write.
Everything. Anything. A journalist. Once. Years and years ago. No. Not right
now. Years ago, I was a translator. Writing? Not any more. Translations.
From English. French. German. How? Comics. Magazines. Comik-books.
Batman. Donalduck. Pocketbooks. Yes. Yes. They were cheaper, you know.
Yes, dictionaries. Yeah, I read English. Shakespear. I don't pronounce it well.
Never cared to learn. No, there was nobody to teach me how to say it right. I
say "guater" and it is "water". My eight-year old says so.

No. I don't speak French. Not a word. All right, if you say so: monsiú. . . No,
I cannot pronounce French well. Books don't include pronunciation in any
language. . . Any language, you know? (Smokes.) What? I am sorry. . . (Kills

the cigarette against the sole of his shoe.) No. I did not see the sign. All right.
I saw it. Very nervous. I am very nervous. Well, all right, I thought this was a
free country! (Puts another cigarette in his mouth. He does not light it.)
The beginning? Bueno. . . I was born in 1937. . . Not so far back? My father
died in 1957. . . No? Let's see, where would you have me start? How did I
come?

COUP

(Enrique changes the typewriter's position. Now the table is his desk.
Combat noises far away. A machine gun. Howitzers. Voices. Enrique types
quickly. Drinks from a bottle. Writes violently. Stops. Stands up. Walks
around. Opens his shirt. Tucks in the sleeves. Holds his head with his hands.
Sits. Types. Looks far away and listens.)
They were dying! Murdered! Slaughtered! (Types a few words.) They were
dying, and I had nothing, nothing at all! Only paper, a typewriter and a bottle.
. . I wanted to write. I wanted to fight in my own way, but I could not. I could
not write! I sweated, I cried, I suffocated! I was looking at them dying in
front of my window and I wanted to write everything. I wanted to note each
sacrifice, each crime, each murder; everything, so that they would be
immortal. Immortal from the very minute of their death, but I could not. I
could not! I could not rescue them from their death!
(Hits the table with both hands. Stands up. Walks again in desperation.
Listens. The noises go on. Women, yelling. A cannon. He covers his ears.)
Enough! Enough, enough, enough! My God, My Dear God, Save my people;
save my people, Oh, God! But, if I will never. . .
(Holds the bottle and drinks. Trembles. Listens. The fighting fades away.
Enrique opens his eyes wide in desperation. Hides his head in his hands.)

They are defeated! They are lost! They are dead!

(Drops on the chair. Hides his face in his hands. His arms on his legs. He does not move while the fight and the noises fade.)

Yolanda - Enrique? Are you there? What are you doing? Run. . . Run! There is still time! They will come for you now. . . Now, when everything is over once again, they will come! You know how it is. Enrique? You are drinking. . . You are drunk. . .

Enrique - Hey? No. . . No. . . It's all right. . . (Cleans his face) Yolanda? Is that you?

Yolanda - You must go away, Enrique! They are coming. They are coming now. They will come as they always come. . . In the night, in silence, the killers. The killers. . . To kill you, to harm us. You must go away. You must flee right away!

Enrique - But no, no. . . Not now. . . They will not come. . . yet. There are others. So many. Others, first. . . Tell me: do you really believe?. . .

Yolanda - Run, run! Leave now!

Enrique - (Takes two steps. Rises his lapels. Hesitates.) It is raining. Such a torrential rain. . . It's raining like hell!

Yolanda - Go, go away. We'll pray for you. God has always been kind to us. He has always taken care of us. God will help us once again. Go.

Cecilia - Go, Dad. Go away, please! Don't worry about us. God will help. . . us.

Alejo - We will be all right, Dad. Everything is going to be all right. Take care, please. Take care of yourself. Don't forget us, Father!

Vera - You will come back, Daddy, right? You have to come back, right? Just a few days, Mother said, a few days. I'll pray for you, Daddy. I'll pray always. Every day, always. Always. When you come back, I'll tell you about my dreams, all my dreams, okay? (Wails.)

(Enrique looks around, searching for his enemies. Three steps. Hand in a pocket. A gun. He hesitates. Looks back. Exit left.)
(Pause.)

THE SKIN

(Enter right. Walks to the table. He is tired. Looks around.)

Ranger - Halt! Who goes there? Halt, I say! (A shot.)

Enrique - (On his knees next to the table.) Oh, My God, My God. . . Please, hide me. . . Please, please God, help me. . . Help me. . . For my wife, for my children's sake. . . My little children. . . (Motionless. Waits. He sits. Lays his head on the table. Pause.)

(Silence.)

(A baby "talks," laughs, cries. Enrique shakes his head. He lays it again on the table. Tries not to listen. The baby cries. Enrique raises his head.)

Enrique - My victimizers. . . And my victims. (Listens. Shrugs his shoulders. Acknowledges the baby. To the audience.) His name is Enrique, like mine. I never saw him as a child. I wasted half my life without knowing he was there. When he was born, the right of First Night, el derecho de pernada, was law. It had been changed a little, but it was common. Quite common.

Teacher - An invention of the Conquistadores, we still honor the right of First Night, our right to deflower every maiden at her first wedding night.

Priest - It is like a character blemish. Like drinking. A venial sin.

Professor - Like being lazy. A defect, no more. Like a big, ugly nose.

Policeman - It is not a crime. Not illegal.

Enrique - I did not know he had been born. And, when I saw him, I could not believe he was there. I could not believe he was mine. . . I could not believe. . . It was the skin.

Enrique Peñaranda - The skin is our first circumstance.

Tupac Katari - Our first law.

Voices - We are racists, you know. Racists, we are!

Indian Man - So much so, that we have never heard about racism. We don't know what it is.

Enrique - I am less of a half-breed because I am whiter, but we have people who are less of a mestizo because they are more copper-skinned. I am too white to be thought a mestizo, and I am not a bit copper-skinned. But I am a half blood. I am a white half-breed, that is, a mestizo rejected by the copper-skinned because I am white and by the very white because I am not as white as. . . That is, I am almost copper-skinned, I mean, half-breed, but. . .

Professor - The white man, the copper-man, and the mestizo fight a perennial battle inside each body, each eye, each hand, each cell. . .

Germán Busch - Besides fighting between themselves always. Always. . .

Graduate Student - Each man, each woman, each child is a lethal battleground for the copper-skinned man, the white man, and the half-breed, the copper-white man.

Worker - The past, the present and the future. . .

Old Man - Yes. . . But, which is which?

Doctor - The mix of bloods is not finished yet. It can never end. . .

Secretary - Which will win? Who will triumph?

Enrique - In this specific case. . . Kiko. . . Yes, we call him Kiko, because nobody would dare to compare him with Don Enrique, that's me, I myself, or much less would anybody dare to even think about Don Humberto Enrique, who will never be his grandfather even if he was my father. **Priest** - That's how it is. That's right.

Enrique - In this case, I say, the skin set him apart because he had his father's clear eyes but his mother's skin. . . A dark skin. . .

Priest - An unforgivable sin.

Lady - Socially speaking, of course.

Judge - Not a crime. . .

Lawyer - Worse than a crime.

Policeman - Each of us lives in his own secluded box. Elbow hitting each other. . .

Miss New Spring - Spying on everybody's shade of the body. . .

Franciscan - And that of the soul. . . The soul's shade too.

Enrique - Because all of this has a proper place too. It is also important, as we will see. Only my nose, this notable nose, allows a general guess that my grandparents'grandparents were Indians. . . Today, we call them campesinos, but in fact they are the defeated, Indians or campesinos. . .

Kiko - The war of the skin is inexorable.

Enrique - From this side. . . I look like one of the Conquistadores' children. . . This profile, this side of my face and my soul allows me certain privileges, certain crimes, great or small, which, if perpetrated while I, seen from this other. . . (Turns around) From this other, darker side, would have brought me a fast and cruel punishment long ago. That is why, if one is born with an almost white profile. . . (Turns) Like this one, one learns very fast to use it as often as possible, because it is a shield against the kicks, the punches and the tortures suffered by others. . . (Turns around) Those who were born with both profiles very American, that is to say, indigenous. . .

Kiko - In one word, defeated.

Enrique - The problem with Kiko. . . He was born with very American profiles, both of them. Slanted eyes, copper face, big cheek bones. . . In another word, an Indian.

Kiko - Indian. Indian! Indian, that's to say, criminal. The Indian's first sin is to be born, because he is born defeated.

Gentleman - Defeated and vanquished always, every time, with every action and every gesture. Defeated everywhere.

Enrique - There must be some time, some place, though, because these have been five centuries already, five long centuries. . .

Francisco Pizarro - It was, thou knowst, that thou were too many. . . Pagan and heathen, yes. But so many!

Diego de Almagro - Until the mines swallowed thee. . . The silver mountain. . . The copper mountain, the golden one. . .

Dominican - It's time for thou to know this: the flesh is weak. . .

Luis Recio de León - And know this: the right of First Night is a law!

School Child - In the early times. . . In the Kollasuyo, we were so happy, all of us. . . They say.

Scholar - Because in the socialist Inca empire. . .

Businessman - That's a lie. Just a lie, I tell you!

Kuraka - Ama Sua. Ama Llulla. Ama Kella.

Scholar - Do not be lazy. Do not tell lies. Do not steal. Simple law.

Indian Shepherd - The Law of the Inca!

Augustinian - Lies! Lies! Old women's lies!

Francisco Pizarro - This way, rascals, to make yourself rich!

Diego de Almagro - Or that way to the peninsula, ruffians, to be poor. . . Misers!

Pedro de Anzúrez - But. . . Listen to me, by the nails of Christ: there is a silver mountain!

Nuflo de Chavez - I swear by my soul's salvation there is a mountain of gold: the Golden Mountain is there! The Great Paititi is down there!

Melchor de Rodas - I swear by the holy cross, the Fountain of Youth is right there, there! Thirty days to Westwind. . .

Martín de Robles -The truth? The truth, you say? There's no truth but silver, you rascal!

Men - Silver! Silver, the silver mountain!

Simón I. Patiño - Members of the Board, there's no more truth than tin!

Worker - No truth but oil! Pass the word to the General Manager!

Drug Lord - Than cocaine, than Mary Jane!

Men - Yellow gold, black gold, green gold!

Men - Silver! Tin! Oil! Coca!

Inquisitor - Fire cleans crimes, heathen, and blood washes sins, barbarians!

Indian Boy - I, a barbarian? I, an innocent forgiven by the great deluge?

Professor - A barbarian, forgotten by History!

Doctor - Barbarian, ignored by progress!

Priest - Barbarian, denied by his own gods!

Military - Copper skin. . . Cannon fodder. . . Skin. . .

Inquisitor - Skin damned forever!

Viceroy Toledo - Bring civilization, progress and faith: burn, burn!

Vasquez de Urrea - Save their souls; destroy, destroy!

Ranger - This is for freedom. Guys, start the Panzers!

Green Beret - We will sow tomorrow!

Businessman - Today is the day of tin, oil and coca!

Men - Amen.

Diplomat - Today is the day of the gunship, the mercenary, napalm!

Men - Amen.

Mercenary - Machine-guns. Fighters. Torture!

Men - Amen.

Chola - Ah! But the mestizo tortures the mestizo!

Worker - The copper-skinned man is killing the copper-skinned man!

Campesino - The white man. . .

Child Shepherd - The white man runs away. . .

Siringa Man - He who looks white, flees.

Baker - He who can disguise himself as a white man, slips away. . .

Child - Why is he fleeing?

Kiko - The skin is the first law.

Military - And the last one!

Admiral - It's war!

Voice -The skin states: this one man can go, he can travel. . . He can live anywhere in the world. . . He may go, if he can, to the empire where the sun never sets. . .

School Child - In his children, go away tomorrow to pay a visit to the moon.

College Student - Go to share the sweet and sour days of the Galaxy. . .

Truck Driver - to sail along time and swim in space. . .

Journalist - To bless with his breathe all eternity. . .

Tourist - Go, walk away, go far and invent other worlds!

Kiko - But the skin states:

Men - This one man, this with the copper-like skin, this one will never go away!

Salesman - Never, because he cannot leave his skin behind.

Secretary - If he leaves, If he ever dares to try and leave, bold and shameless. . .

Mayor - They will haunt him like a dog. They'll shoot at him with everything. . . He'll be like smoke. They'll loath him. They'll reject him. They'll relegate him to loneliness and silence until he goes mad.

Teacher - He won't speak the language of the Galaxies. He won't understand our blessed bread of the primordial Big Bang, or anything about anything. He will understand nothing, he won't say a word. . .

Foreman - Like fish on sand, he will perish, if he does not come back.

Rancher - If he does not come back very soon.

Businessman - He will come back, because he is a monster out there.

Teacher - A strange worm who babbles an alien language, strange mores, with eyes in the back of his head that can only look backwards, backwards to the ghost of dead centuries.

College Student - That is also true, twenty dead centuries!

Scholar - Twenty centuries of glories forever forgotten; webs of vanity on twenty centuries denied and forgotten. . .

Military - The skin states: this one man does not go; he is a dirty copper-skinned ghost. . .

Trader - A forever defeated pariah, rag born already dead, a ghost that could never understand his defeat, his vanquish, his humiliation for five centuries. .

Kiko - This man, the copper-man, condemned to stay forever, breathless in his grave of winds, cold and violence. . .

Men - Forever!

Mallcu - In his burnt jungle, in his devastated woods, in his empty plains, his desolate valleys, his poisoned rivers. . . In my sacked world of snow and wind, hunger and silence. . .

        HOUNDS

Enrique - (Claps his hands) It is a mess. A real mess. It is also the truth. If one manages to kill the voices that talk to us from our own veins, everything is clear and simple: some among us can go, we try to go and . . . Well, we go.

Children - They go.

Enrique - Some, those with a dark skin, they cannot go because they cannot even begin to read this century of wonders. . .

Radio Announcer - This century of the supersonic, the computer, the hermaphrodite.

Enrique - (Shakes his head, rejecting these voices.) Enough. It's enough. In this quagmire of uncertainties, the worst of it is that nobody can breathe but nobody stops breathing, either. . . We stumble, all blind and clumsy, and trip and go nowhere. . .

Mamani - All right. Say it. Now.

Enrique - The voices in my veins tell me that those who are stalking me and smell my blood from the other side of this adobe wall are those who will not go. Those who will never go away. . .

Man - (Tanks in a square.) Those who chose to kill and burn their own blood. . .

Woman - (Military parade.) Those who learned to hate their skin.

Child - That will never go away. . .

Youth - The professional killer of their own blood.

Women - Eternal murderers of their own blood.

Enrique - They. . . Them: the military!

(Darkness. Light.)

(Weapons. Noises. People running. Boots. Voices yelling orders. Armed "medics" and "nurses" with weapons. Faces with operating masks. Torchlights. People walk around Enrique, hidden by an invisible wall.)

Kiko - Find that bastard! A thousand to whoever finds him!

(Enrique is seated on the chair. Elbows on the table. He has a gun. Men come from right.)

Soldier - Here, lieutenant! Here! He is here!

(They hit a door. Noises. Enrique holds his gun. Aims it. He trembles. Almost lying on the table.)

Red Beret - There's nobody there, you scoundrels! Only mice! Rats only!

(Men go away. They exit. Enrique lowers his arms, slowly. Pause.)

(Men enter left. Enrique turns around. Almost lying on his back.)

Sailor - What about this hole? Who has checked this room? He must be here! He has to be here! Here, here!

(Enrique tries to raise his gun. Aims at the voices. Both hands holding the gun. Trembles. Waits.)

Medic - There's nobody there, Rogelio! Nobody. Ask the lieutenant. We better go on!

(Men exit left. Enrique lets his hands hang down. Sighs. Cleans the sweat from his eyebrows. Men enter. Enrique turns around to face them, his back to the audience.)

Civilian with Weapon - Here, boys, here! He has to be here! We have looked everywhere already. There's nowhere else to look for this dog. Open that door!

(Enrique drops on his knees. Raises his arms against the men. Huddled, he waits. Pause.)

Nurse with Weapon - No, man! No. . . He looked inside that room. Him himself. There's nobody there. It's empty. Let's go. Now.

(Men exit. Enrique drops his arms and rests his head on the floor. Silence. Pause. Stands up slowly. Two steps. Sits. Tries to stand up again. He cannot. He trembles. He cannot control himself. Waits. He stands up.)

Enrique - They won't find me. . . Ever. They will never find me. . . Alive.

(Enrique takes two steps. Turns around. Holds his hands. Vomits. Trembles violently. Then, relaxes. He puts his gun in a pocket. Walks to the left. Looks around.)

Mamani - Enrique.

Enrique - (Screams) Never!

Mamani - Be quiet. It's me.

Enrique - Mamani? But. . . What are you doing here?

Mamani - I came to take you away from this mess.

Enrique - (Walks to center. Looking at his shoes.) Nobody can take me away from this. . .(Hesitates.) They are everywhere. . . They stalk me. . . They hound me. . . He wants my hide. . . He needs me.

Mamani - Take it easy. We'll get away from this one, too. (Enrique does not move, still looking at his shoes.) Just walk away. I will cover you. If you need to run, run. What counts is to do it very naturally. Be natural. Don't betray yourself. Don't think about what you are doing. You get me? Walk and think about something nice, really nice. Forget you are yourself and walk inside the embassy. The easiest thing in the world. Do it. Now.

Enrique - But. . . How about you, Mamani?

Mamani - I'll cover you. And then, I'll go inside, too. Don't worry. Nothing will happen. Nobody remembers us. Not yet. There are so many big shots. They are looking for them now.

Enrique - I will walk. . . I will think about something nice. . . Something very nice. . . When? Now?

Mamani - Now! Go! Go!

(Enrique starts walking fast. Three steps.)

Soldier - Halt! Stop there! Stop right there, you dirty dog!

Kiko - Now I got you! You are mine! I have you now!

Enrique - (Turns around) Who's there? Who? You! You. . . (Turns around. Runs. Exit right.)

Mamani - Run! Run!

(Shots. Men running. Yell.)

Soldier - Kill him! Kill that man! Stop right there! Halt!

Kiko - Mamani! I caught you!

Mamani - Never alive, you murderer!

(A shot. Mamani screams in agony. Silence.)

(Pause.)

CAPTURE

Enrique - (Enter left. Runs. Stops. In anguish.) Asylum! Asylum! I demand political asylum!

Ambassador - Good afternoon, Don Enrique!

Enrique - Mister Ambassador!

Ambassador - Relax, now. . . Take it easy, Don Enrique. Your darkest hours are over. Please, do come in.

Enrique - Oh, you are so nice, Mr. Ambassador. Thank you, sir. Thank you very much.

Ambassador - The least I can do, between gentlemen. Those brutal murderers. . .

(Enrique changes his attitude. Relaxed. One hand inside a pocket. A drink in the other. Drinks.)

Ambassador - This may be long, Don Enrique, but, at least, you will be very comfortable here.

Enrique - Oh, thank you very much, Mr. Ambassador.

Ambassador - Have you been in our library before?

Enrique - Well, no. No, Mr. Ambassador.

Ambassador - Please do come in. This is your house.

Enrique - (Two steps. In shadows.) Well, let's see. Let's look at your books, Mr. Ambassador.

(Far away, shots and gunfire. Somebody yells.)

Ambassador - This one is Neruda, Don Enrique. The golden edition. . .

Enrique - Ah, yes. . .(Quotes) I can write the saddest verses tonight. . . (His voice goes softer.)… I can write, for instance. . .

(Sounds of a printing machine.)

Man's Voice - Write, for instance, the truth in two columns, twenty inches and every other day. The power of the printed word.

Enrique - (Strong) I am the voice of the people. I am the truth in two columns and twenty inches every other day.

Editor - Please, stop writing that nonsense. They will make you spit out your soul one of these nights!

Enrique - (Speech strong and loud.) I say it, I write it and I sign it.The true source of this crisis is corruption at the highest levels of this government! (The printing machine stops. Broken doors and windows. Broken glasses. Kicks and shots.)

Editor - (Patient and low) There you are. Now you'll see, to jail.

Reporter - (Quietly.) Yes, and then, to the graveyard.

Doorman - If they don't disappear him, as they did to others.

Enrique - But they cannot do this for one sentence. . . One short sentence! (Enrique seated in front of the table. A light blinds him. He is interrogated.)

Atlas - Who the hell wrote this shit! What son of a dirty mother wrote this piece of dung?

Enrique - I. I wrote it. . . But, it is the truth!

(Darkness. Kicks and punches. Laughter. Cries. Shadows.)

Atlas - The truth, hey? (Laughter) How about this truth? Are you going to write about this truth? Would your lordship wish to write a few lines about this truth, too? Well, have your truth! How do you like it? Enjoy it! (Punch. A cry.) Learn this truth! (An electric machine. Flashes of light. A cry. Pause. Darkness.)

(Weak light.)

Enrique - (Lying across the table.) I fear nothing in this world more than torture. . . My skin is a coat of flames. . . Flames behind my eyes. Flames inside my head. . . My eyes. . . In the dark, one finds out that one eye, my own eye. . . But they could not do this to me. . . They could not do anything to me, because I am the voice of the people. . . I write. I write, and everybody looks at me with respect, with consideration. They are afraid of the people. . . (Light. Lying face up on the table. Arms and legs open. Face covered by black blood. Raises his head.)

Who's there? Who's there? (Tries to look around.) Who are you? Don't touch me! Please, don't touch me! Don't touch my eyes! Don't touch my hands! (Drops his head. Rises his head again.) I am thirsty. . . Thirsty. . . Please help me. . . Who are you? Whoever you are, please help me. . . My eyes, my hands! They have broken my hands. They have. . . My eyes, my eyes! Just for one sentence. . . Just for a sentence, such a short sentence. . . My eyes! They have burnt my eyes! Oh, My God. . . (on the table, defeated.) (Pause.)

Daniel - Don Enrique. . . I have brought a paper. . .

Enrique - Yolanda? Yolanda? My poor Yolanda! God bless them. . . My children. . . Did you see my children?

Daniel - No, Don Enrique. . . Just a piece of paper. . .

Enrique - Oh, please. . . Please. . .

Yolanda - (Off. While she talks, Enrique huddles up.) "Our very dear Enrique: We are all praying for you. Nobody tells us where you are, or if you are still alive, but I know we will be together once again. Have faith, Enrique. We are well. I am proud of my children, your children. I cannot write any more now. A kiss. Yolanda."

Enrique - (Rises his head) Yolanda. . . Yolanda. . . Proud. . . My children. . . My children. . . My eyes! You scoundrels, my eyes! My eyes! (Falls from the table. On his knees.)

Loayza - But we are very generous. Generous patriots.

Benavidez - You are so lucky you can choose.

Enrique - I can choose? Choose? What can I choose?

Loayza - Everything is in your hands, you damn fool!

Benavidez - You write another word. . .

Loayza - Another word, just another word. . . And then, it won't be your neck only!

Benavidez - Everybody dies! Everybody! Understand, you imbecile?

Enrique - My. . . My family? You mean. . .? My. . .?

Loayza - All of you!

Enrique - Death and torture. . . Or my silence?

Loayza - Your absolute silence!

Enrique - But they are innocent!

Loayza - Nobody is innocent!

Enrique - Their lives in exchange of my silence. . .

Benavidez - Or the graveyard for you and for your. . . precious children!

Loayza - Do you understand it now, you idiot?

Enrique -   (Seated in front of the table. Defeated. Looks at the audience.) I understand. I did not understand it before, because I could not believe it. I understand. . . now.

I understood every word, I understood the danger. I dreamt about it a thousand nights. Not only my death. . . Not only my slow death under torture, but their death, their pain. . . I chose. I chose silence. My life became ashes and my eyes remained burnt and clouded. I did not write any more. I did not publish anything else. (Pause) They killed me.

(Pause.)

STRUGGLE

Yolanda - You drink too much, Enrique. Take care of yourself.

Enrique - All right, I drink.

(Holds a bottle and drinks. Seated at the table. Aymara music. Stands.) I drink, I dance, I do not think, I do not talk. I drink. I do not write. I dance. When we dance in the squares, in the streets, in the graveyards and in the immense frozen deserts of our world. . . (Dances.)

We dance like this. It is very easy, because it is elemental. It is primordial, this pentatonal music. Prior to the deluge. We dance like this because we dance God's youth. His childhood. Our childhood. This eternal childhood. We are children when we dance. Children, dancing our pure joy of living. It is a simple joy, a joy. . . A very sour joy. (Stops.) An anguished joy. A desperate joy without words, so that our hopes may never die, ever. We dance nights and days, days and nights, we never stop. We fill our bellies and our heads with alcohol and with music and we dance, we dance, we dance, we fall asleep while dancing and we just fall on the dust of our narrow little streets made of stones and moonlight. (Drops on the floor.)
(From the floor.)

This is a sour joy, anguished and sadder than death itself, because we are slaves. Slaves through centuries, nailed to this tough land as to a holy wooden cross. Slaves of a thousand hundred mirages.
(On his knees.)

But the struggle goes on. It is an eternal struggle, a struggle born with this music. A struggle made of incredible feats of heroism. Fought by naked men, men without weapons, without voices, without echoes, gods or flags. . . Forgotten as we are by our gods, whoever those gods may be. . .
(Standing.)

It is a blind struggle. Fought by the most pure ideals against the most pure ideals. Only ideals of such a divine purity can make titans and heroes like my heroes: nobody indoctrinates them, nobody catechizes them, nobody opens a window to human communion for them. . . My nameless heroes, rejected by their renegade god, sit at the their hut doors to drink and to smell the fury and the power of their rebellion and to watch the setting of the sun, a sun forever alien. . .

They dream this world as it should have been, not as it is in fact, and they reject this absurd and constant nightmare, they go after their beautiful dream, a dream that they will never give away. . . It is with that power and that fury that they walk after their overpowering vision and deliver their meager flesh to torture, to rape, to fire and to the hatred of their enemies. That's how they have lived for five centuries and how they have built a white rainbow with their bones, an arch which begins in their shafts, goes around the globe to end in their tin huts. . . Their hunger, their heroism and their senseless death are the offerings made by this century to its gods of gold and tin, drugs and death.

(Opens his arms.)

They are the campesinos. Rooted to the land in woods, jungles and plains, they make their daily offering to the barbarous god who blesses other lands and deprives them of the bread they sow, takes away from them woods, grains, skins and nails till they lack the strength to care for their seed.

But they struggle. They will struggle till the end of time.

They are the workers. Broken by a sordid routine, by the perennial hammering of foreign machines and by poisonous smokes and dusts, muzzled by perpetual shadows, they never wear the cloth they spin and weave, they never see but a thin piece of bread on their humble table, they surrender everything to the barbarous god who blesses other lands and assigns them their fate of dying daily, dying naked, alone and desperate, victims of a vain rebellion against their renegade god.

But they struggle. They will struggle till the end of time.

They are the miners. Nailed under the earth a thousand fathoms deep as an eternal offering to the barbarous god who blesses other lands, other mountains, other works, other glories, they never see the steely glitter of the metal they dig with their naked hands, they never have enough strength left to care for their seed.

But they struggle. They will struggle till the end of time.
(Arms across his chest.)

My life came from their death. I feel them and I see them right here, inside my heart. I live the bottomless depth of their contradictions, I feel their immense anguish of knowing that we are forever rejected in the banquet of the centuries. I know how hard it is to see ourselves as dead leaves feeding the glut of other people, people we have never met, people we have never seen, people who never wanted to shake our hands. How could I not understand them?

They live in me. I feel them. I hear them. They are mine. They cry and they yell. They speak through me. I am the screech of their anguish. I am the broken outcry of their sadness. . . I am the scream of their suffering. . . I am. . . I am, too, part of that land, a drop of those waters, another eye under the sun in the plateau. . . I am, and it is with the humblest pride that I say this, also a tiny part of that people.

MASSACRE

Voices - (Far away.) The people . . . united. . .will never be defeated!
College Student - Freedom! Liberty! Freedom!
School Child - Free Elections!

Employee - Democracy! Democracy!

Worker - Liberty! Democracy! Free Elections!

Voices - (Choir.) The people. . . united. . .will never be defeated!

Enrique - One day. The sun rose. It rose for three days, but it did rise.

Taylor - There are only two roads for the generals!

Butcher - To serve the people, to be a part of their people. . .

Woman Baker -. . .or to be their people's murderers forever!

Driver - Their people's executioners forever!

Campesino - Forever!

Old Woman - Murderers, killers, slayers!

Voices - (Choir.) The people. . . united. . .will never be defeated!

(The same chant until voices vanish in the distance.)

Enrique - (Listens and repeats it.) The people. . . United... Will never be defeated! The people. . . united. . . (Hesitates.) Three days later, the sun set once more. The people, united, were defeated. The people were defeated in the streets. In the squares they were defeated. In the parks, in their homes, in their men they were defeated. They were defeated in their young women's virtue; in their childrens' innocence they were defeated.

The people, united, were defeated. The people were machine-gunned in their factories. They were massacred in their plains, they were beheaded in their valleys, they were tortured and decimated in their mines. The people's defeat was no secret: every newspaper in the world mentioned this defeat. Every short wave broadcast spoke about it, every channel had it in sound, voice, noise and color for each seven o'clock report at dinner time. Three thousand men, women and children were killed.

Woman Teacher - It was a three-day war of tanks and cannons against naked chests.

Priest - It was a genocidal operation under the frozen stars, against the silence of the world.

Old Man - Human consciences also dope themselves, the big fish eats the small fish, and there is no more law.

Enrique - On the third day, the sun turned itself off.

Women - (The women will read the following text as a prayer. The pictures will be men, women and children in the mines, in the mining camps, parades and festivals among the miners, miners in the shafts, all trying to underline their human qualities.)

The commando attacked Caracoles with cannons, howitzers, tanks and war planes.

Our men fought with sticks, stones and a few dynamite charges.

The miners were exterminated and those who survived fled to the hills.

The soldiers chased them and killed the men inside the mine.

They caught some and tortured some and many were impaled with long knives.

The wounded were also beheaded.

They forced a miner to chew a dynamite stick and they blew him in pieces.

They whipped children with electrical wires and they forced them to eat black powder.

Young boys were forced to lay on broken glass and we women were then forced to walk on them.

Then the soldiers walked on their bodies, too.

The army attacked us like crazy dogs because they were drugged and they did not hesitate to rape us, to rape girls and even children.

They killed sheep, chicken, pigs, men, women and children.

They took the dead and the wounded in their trucks.

They forbade us women to search for our dead and to dig a grave for them.

"Not allowed," they said.

And when we could get near to the site, we found only shirts, coats, shoes and pants soaked in blood.

Our dead had disappeared.

They had thrown them in a trench behind the cemetery and they did not allow us to identify or to wash our dead.

Andrés Villca, our kuraka, went crazy.

Woman Miner - Our people, united, was defeated.

(Darkness. Pause. Light.)

Enrique - (Stands in front of the table.) This time, I could hardly say good-bye to my children. They were searching for me like wolves, like crazy predatory beasts. . .

Soldier - (Shadow on the wall.) Who wrote that shit, you piece of dung?

Sailor - (Shadow on the wall.) Who says we are our people's killers?

Ranger - (Shadow on the wall.) Who damned our honor?

Red Beret - (Shadow on the wall.) Who has dirty words for our love for this land?

Kiko - (Shadow on the wall.) Find that drop of shit!

Policeman - (Shadow on the wall.) A thousand for his hide!

Enrique - (Lowers his head. Looks at the audience.) They will never find me. They will never catch me. . . alive. I fear nothing in this world more than torture. (Holds his head in his hands.)

EXILE

Ambassador - Don Enrique. . .

Enrique - Yes? Yes. . . Here.

Ambassador - Congratulations, Don Enrique! Your papers are here! You are a free man!

Enrique - (Motionless.) Free at last?

Ambassador - Free at last. I myself will take you to your plane.

Enrique - (Motionless.) Thank you, Mr. Ambassador. (Stands up. Walks around.) Free! Free. Free? Free. . . What for? Where to go, now? To what corner of the world? Of the world, so alien and so wide? Free. Free? Who wants to be free. . . Like this? (Pause.) I want to be free. I must be free. It is my duty to be free. It is my fate to be free, because I have not finished my work. No. No and no. I must begin again. (Accepts his situation. His hand over his head. Straightens up. Assumes an almost heroic posture.)

Ambassador - And now. . . Where to, Don Enrique?

Enrique - Where? Where? How do I know, my friend? You open roads by walking!

Ambassador - Ah, this Don Enrique! Have you been away before? I mean, in foreign countries?

Enrique - This is my fourth exile.

Ambassador - Your fourth exile? But. . . What a man!

Enrique - This is my fate, don't you see? My fate. . . Never a shelter. Never a day of peace, a sunny day in peace. I am a tired traveler, a wanderer. . . Besides, I must go on. My work is not done.

Ambassador - Go with luck, Don Enrique!

Enrique - God rides with me!

(Sits. Looks around, lost.)

(Pause.)

(Noise of crowd.)

Enrique - (Puts a cigarette in his mouth. Does not light it. Turns around, looks across the table.) That's how I came. A long road, full of suffering and pain. But here I am. I was lucky. Bad luck for you, if you wish. I slept in the plane because I had not slept well for a long time. I woke up here. I ask for political asylum. I am a legitimate refugee. And I have not finished my work. (Crosses his arms, almost indifferent. A typewriter's sound. Stamps on the table. Stands up. Polite.) Thank you. Of course. I will be back. In a month. (Turns around and walks away. Stands.) Free? Free. Who wants to be free, like this? ¿Where am I? ¿Where are my children? ¿Where should I go? I have lost everything. Not even my shadow is mine anymore. Free? Who wants to be free like this? (Pause) I. I want to be free. I must be free. I must continue with my work. (Exit right. Enter left. Sits at the table. Gets ready to type.) I will try again. . . I will begin once again. . . I will chase my. . . My. . . How did my dear child call them? What was that word she made?

Vera (Voice) - Dad. . . Daddy. . . Let me tell you my dreamhopes. . . All my dreamhopes. . .

Yolanda (Voice) - What is it, Doctor? What is it?

Vera (Voice) - My dreams. . . hopes… For my Dad…

Enrique - This night is mine. . . Mine. Mine alone. A whole night for myself and my dreams and my hopes. . . (Begins to type.)

Yolanda (Voice) - He spoiled her. . . She misses him so much!

Doctor (Voice) - Where is her father, Doña Yolanda?

Yolanda (Voice) - Abroad. . . In exile.

Vera (Voice) - My Dad. . . Daddy. . . Where is Daddy? I want to tell him my dreams, my hopes, all my hopes. . .

Enrique - (Stops.) My dreams, my hopes, all my hopes. . . Let's see. . .

(Reads.) It's not bad. . . Bad. . . It's not. . . (Writes. Stops. Reads.) No. No.
No! It's wrong! (Reads.) I don't like it. It's wrong. It was not like this. It's
not strong enough. It is not what I wanted to say. It's not written as I wanted
to write it. It's false. It's weak. It's dead. It's false, false. . . Let's see. (Writes.
Reads. Writes.) I don't remember now how it was. How it was, really. . . It
was not like this. This is not. . . This cannot be. . . (Writes. Reads. Writes.
Stops and backs off.) It was not like this. How was it? I saw it a hundred
times! I felt it every time! It needed only to be written! (Reads.) But this is
not how it was. This. . . This. No, no, no! A thousand times, no!
But. . . Will I ever be able to do something better than. . . this? (Stands up.
Walks around.) Once again, but only this? Only this. . . This. . . spiderweb,
once again? But, what torture is this? Why is it that I. . . Why me?
(Hesitates. Stares to the audience. Hesitates. In anguish.)

        That 's it. That's it! Why me?

        Why was I born like this? Why me? Why am I nothing but a monkey
with stones in his mouth? A damned choked monkey in search of his own
voice in the storm, an anguished monkey who can guess in a flash the square
of the circle but then cannot but stammer, spit, regurgitate, but never roar. . .
Who vomits nothing but foam, a black foam, when he howls? Why am I like
this? What punishment is this? What was my crime? What, my sin? (Holds
his face in his hands.) Some people fight, some cry. A few kill, when life
strangle them. I write. I write. I write always. Everyday I write. I write. . .
this. Only to write, I have lived so many lives. To be a witness. To offer my
testimony. I was a sailor, a beggar, a worker, a dishwasher I was. . . I was. . . I
was. . . an alien, in one word. An exile. An exile from my country, from life,
from the world, only to write, only to write. . .

        But, how long is this painful balance between a groan and a smile?
Who can live like this, hanging forever from a weak tread of absurdity? I

used my life to see people dying for just causes, heroic causes. . . I am a witness. I could see justice in their causes, but I am not a man of action. I never took those causes as mine. . . The human drama was not written for me to live it, but for me to copy it. . . To copy it with all of its passion, all of its love, all of its hate and fury. . . To catch it alive! Alive, alive! Alive and throbbing, as I feel it in my heart. . .

And my dead. . . Their dying stopped the universe, when my dead died. . . They are legitimate, my dead! My dead, who go on dying because I only write this foam. . . I die their death every night, I smell their last breath, I cry their crying and they come back and live in me, my dead. I dissolve their death in a thousand nights spent remembering, pondering and wondering, along lonely walks on empty streets, along endless monologues, amid anguish and pains to understand, to remember, to fix in my papers, at last, what I have seen, what I have lived, what they have suffered. . . And to offer a small hope built on their death for those who will come, those who will be born tomorrow. . .

I lived their lives, I witnessed their deaths. They are here. I have them with me. Why, then, are they nothing but black foam when I bring them to my papers? Why is it that my heroes and my scoundrels were never able to be born? Why are they never alive? Why was there never heroism or greatness, glory or crime among my specters, the ghosts of my dreams and my hopes? Why is it that I am never able to give them a semblance of life, the breathe which makes a man from any memory, a man for whom all men may care, a man who can be respected, can be appreciated. . . Can be, yes. . . Can be loved?

(Head down. Goes back to the table. Looks at his works.)

And if I stop, if I desist when I lose this veil from my eyes and can recognize this foam and I throw it away. . . then I find the other face of this particular crime: I cannot abandon it. I will never abandon it. When I try to leave it behind me, I stop living. I stop eating and sleeping. I deny myself to human dealings. I wear myself out like a wild animal. I hate silence and I hate noise. I damn. I hate God. I drink and dissipate in nights of vice and desperation. My ghosts haunt me. My dreams and hopes torture me.

This wound hurts, bleeds and stings. It burns! It burns, it bites and it forces me, in loneliness and silence, among hopes and anguish, vertigo and fevers, to sit again in front of this paper, this white paper, hostile and indifferent like the chasm of night, to once again stitch my voice without an echo, perennially damned as I am by absurdity. . . Foam, foam, everything is foam for me!

Here they are, then. They come, demand, urge and yell. They sigh, moan, roar in the dark of night, and they even cast their accusations: (Points at the darkness, accusing an accuser that shouts at him.)

VICTIMS AND VICTIMIZERS

Mamani - Wounds, none! Torture, never!

Enrique - (Shakes his finger.) You saved me! You saved me! Why did you save me?

Mamani - I admired you. . . I could die just once, you could kill death!

Enrique - How can you know?

Mamani - It was enough for me to. . .

Enrique - Well, let it be enough! I asked you nothing. I said nothing. You chose your path. . . And your death!

Mamani - But now: write! Speak, now! If you don't speak, we all die with you!

(Enrique shudders. Shakes. Suffers his guilt. Runs to the table. Holds a "paper." Shows it high. Picks another "paper." Another. And another.)

Enrique - But. . . I write! Don't you see that I write? (Holds "papers" in both hands.) I write! I write always! But everything comes out death, sterile, false.

Woman - (Enrique turns his head, shocked.) I loved you. I gave you my love and my life. I was all acquiescence. For this. . . I loved you?

Enrique - You too? But. . . If you. . . (Shakes his head.) You should be happy with what I left you. I left you more than what I left to the whole world. I left you everything! Everything!

Woman - And a son.

Enrique - (Head down, guilty.) I knew too late.

Woman - You know she died.

Enrique - Too late. . .

Woman - You know I died.

Enrique - I was told too late! I was writing. . . I was traveling, looking around, trying to remember. . . I was recording, taking notes, watching. . . (He cuts himself short. Looks at the audience. Shakes shoulders.) It is not easy. It is not easy to bring you all to spend this afternoon together. It is expensive. It was so expensive! I paid with my blood for this! (Points at his leg.) This leg carries a wound the size of a golden doubloon!

Juan Carlos - You did it yourself!

Enrique - It was him! It was him!

Fernando - You are a coward!

Enrique - Not true!

Roberto - You never knew what real danger was!

Enrique - (Shakes his pointing finger.) You talk too much!

Anita - You left your friends to die!

Enrique - I could not run faster. I have no breath to. . . I smoke too much. They asked me to leave them there. . . To try and live!

Julio - None came back!

Enrique - But they are alive. . . in me! And if I manage to write. . .

Mamani - Write, then!

Enrique - Oh how heavy is this cross, how cruel, how merciless. . .

(A short, mocking laugh cuts him.)

What? Somebody is laughing? Somebody deems himself alien?

Those are foreign dead people, those dead, he says?

Those are fictitious agonies, he points out, and he holds his guts happily, looking at the world while it goes by?

Nothing can change those deaths, he thanks, and the world will forever be the world, he remembers? Besides, he takes some consolation, there's nothing we can do, he says?

Thank God, he chooses, that smoky shadow up there. . . (Points at himself) ...Up here, is just a voice without an echo, a mute shriek, he tries to believe?

He's just a speck in my eyes, somebody says?

But then, what is this dark anguish that shrieks in every chest? Ah, but nobody is innocent any more! Each bullet in the wind wakes a thousand echoes in the Universe! Each death flowers in an assassin and a million accomplices! To close our eyes? To tie our hands? To shut our ears with sounds, songs, shrieks? To deny, to drink, to touch, eat, taste drugs? It's impossible. Nothing will work any more. There's no place to hide. Nobody is innocent now. Executioners all, we all had this appointment tonight, accomplices all. It was not chance, no. It was those voices. Those voices that whisper among distant dog barks in the night, that make silence of our hopes, sand of our victories. It is that shriek behind every clangor, that talks to us about far agonies, distant crimes, deaths and torments we hurl around with our cynical indifference. Those endless crimes of our complicity, our silence

and our blindness. . . The voices of the nameless victims that our guilty heart
claims... and the voices of our victimizers. . .

Kiko - (Cuts him.) A thousand for that bastard!

ENEMIES

Enrique - Oh, shut up, Kiko! (Pause.) Yes, it's Kiko. He was born when I
was 14, and I am 43 now. So, you can figure it out. I could leave one day, so I
left. He could never leave, will never have the power to leave. Never,
because that's the law of the skin. So he chose that road. He is a professional
of crime, a master of torture, a virtuoso of pain. He killed a man tied inside a
jute bag with a cane. He pushes the head of his beer bottles inside women's
genitals. He makes queens of militiamen.

Kiko - I am God's hate, am I?

Enrique - (Hesitates.) He's the dark master of those cells. He beheads them
and leaves the heads early in the morning on the sidewalk, next to every
church. . .

Kiko - I am God's wrath, no?

Enrique - Only he knows where every desaparecido... Only he knows. . .
each grave. . . each nameless grave. . . He is. . . the master of fear and agony.

Kiko - I am the world's conscience, right?

Enrique - Torturer. . . Torturer. . . Torturer!

Kiko - A torturer made by the daily torture of hunger.

Enrique - Murderer. . . Heartless murderer of. . .

Kiko - I lacked finesse. I could never learn it. We cannot all fight with white
gloves and words. . . Sweet words, burning words. . . Deadly words.

Enrique - You torment and hurt. . . You burn, you destroy, you harm. . .

Kiko - Your words make heroes, but your heroes kill. They kill until I kill them. You make heroes, I make martyrs. But they are the same.

Enrique - My works cannot kill. They are nothing but words. Words only.

Kiko - How many did you send against me, with your words as weapons?

Enrique - Words? Just foam, foam only. . . Gripes, no more. . . Dead words. .

Kiko - Right, and with your words they came to kill and I sent them back to you, dead, you visionary of a thousand impossible ways to happiness, you preacher with an empty heart.

Enrique - Kiko, it is torture. . . Torture. . .

Kiko - It's cold outside. It freezes. It freezes always. Outside, men die on their feet, laying against the stones, asleep and frozen. That's what you left me. That and hunger. Someone else's suffering was better. I had nothing to choose. I love life, and to live one must kill.

Enrique - I never harmed anybody, never.

Kiko - You never saw them dying. They held your name. They prayed with your words. They howled, but they told about the universe you made up, so beautiful, teeming of dignity and justice. . . Sometimes, while dying, they damned you when they finally learned that there's no universe but mine, than our universe, yours and mine. They were your victims, too. But they were my enemies, always. Life is war. I am a warrior. I kill with iron and with fire. . .

Enrique - Iron and fire against children. Fire and iron against naked men, defenseless men. Fire and iron against women and old people. Your enemies are the innocent always, the naked. . . Naked and humble people. . . You "glorious" warrior.

Kiko - I have only one weapon: terror. . . We are very few, just a fistful. But we are invincible if we ride the horses of terror. . . Almost immortal. . .

Enrique - But full of hate, these black seas of hate that you sow every day. . .

Kiko - I learned hate. I was not always the black prince of terror, you know that. Without hate, how can one learn to kick and hurt prisoners? I learned that your heroes fear nothing but hate. Only with hate they respect me, only when they learn about my hate. I can never turn my back, because then I can smell theirs, and hate stinks. I carry a bite of their hate on my hand. . . The brand new hate of a child, eleven years old, can you believe it?

Enrique - It was not hate. It was desperation. Terror. Yes, it was terror.

Kiko - No. It was hate. The same hate I carried in my heart when I was eleven. . . At eleven, one is not a pup any more, one is a dog. Or a wolf, if one finds the guts. No. It was hate. It is hate. The hate we find we need in order to survive. We find nothing else. I can feel it: hate burns in me. It flowers and blooms my world. It forces the war of the skin on us: it's me or them. I win because I am absolute: outside myself there's nothing. Nothing exists, nothing can be. Nothing is. And they. . . They are nothing.

Enrique - They are innocent!

Kiko - Nobody is innocent. Are you innocent?

Enrique - My hands are not dirty. . .

Kiko - My hunger carries your name. I still remember the cold, the fear, the loneliness and the sorrows that haunted a child. . . The child I was once.

Enrique - I was told too late.

Kiko - And I did not choose blindness. . . I am not a coward.

Enrique - It was too late. And she said you were dead. . .

Kiko - She could not live. She could not work. She could not read. Nobody was willing to give her a job. She could not clean latrines and take care of a child at the same time. Not here. . . She was forced to choose. No, in fact, she chose nothing. She did what I did. She loved life. She left me back in the barracks, to play with bayonets. . .

Enrique - But she loved you. She was your mother; she must have loved you.

Kiko - How? She never knew me. She did not know who I was. Nobody has a face as a newborn. . .

Enrique - But of course. . . She loved you. She must have loved you.

Kiko - No. I would have been different. No. She had no time to love me. She was alone, and she was nobody. Nothing. She was hungry. She was cold. She was scared. I know. I can recognize them. They are my old enemies. Everything goes to placate them. . . I know. It is simple. I understand her. I understood her always, from the day I met hunger. . . Do you know that I eat well three times a day only since I was made a colonel?

Enrique - Not only with bread. . .

Kiko - Don't start with those noises again. . . Don't abuse my tiredness. . . Don't forget where you are. Don't forget who you face. Don't forget who are you. . . or who I am.

Enrique - I remember, almost blind, after that incident in your cells. . .

Kiko - You couldn't choose silence then, either. You talk. You talk always. You talk now, you preach. . .

Enrique - It's because I believe in that new universe. Everything must change. . . One day...When. . .

Kiko - How can you believe that? You have never done anything for that false universe, that impossible universe of yours.

Enrique - With my words, I. . . I sow the seeds.

Kiko - Your words blind people. They make men deaf. They see nothing, they hear nothing, they only go after their dreams. . . Your martyrs never know what they are doing. They whine until they die, but they cannot learn anything. They shriek until they lose their minds, but they can never learn that the universe is meaningless. . . Poor fanatics of impossible dreams, of some other harmonious universe, of worlds with bread, compassion and justice. Your texts are your crimes, your crimes stitched in syllables. Your dreams sow violence. You send them and I kill them because, if I did not kill

them, they'd come back. They would come back. . . And they come back. . .
Always.

Enrique - You kill. . .

Kiko - You send them; they come in your name. You kill too.

Enrique - You are a murderer!

Kiko - You are terrified, and do not dare to look at the eyes of your victims.

Enrique - My hands are not dirty.

Kiko - Your hands are empty. You never believed anything. You trust
nobody. Your heart is made of cold water. Your own ghosts scare you. Your
get dizzy with your own singsong. You are a shadow, a weak moan in this
thunder. . . You are blind and you burn the eyes of your victims with the fire
of your visions, your false visions. . . You send them against me...
Against me. . . I am your son, don't ever forget it.

Enrique - You are an assassin, Kiko!

Kiko - Assassin, you say? Tell me, there were times when I wondered: when
was the day, the minute when you chose to kill the child I once was? When
and how did you murder me?

Enrique - I don't know you. You are a stranger.

Kiko - Because I waited for you for so long, I let hope die. And I have no
water in my veins.

Enrique - I hate the uniforms, I am terrified by torture. I am afraid of your
shadow, I am terrified by your cells. . . I am a man who tried to educate
himself, I have feelings, I have taste. . .

Kiko - How could I hope for so much, and hope for so long, hope for this
miracle, this tiny daily miracle that could have changed everything?

Enrique - You haunted me. You stalked me always, you took pleasure in
hurting me. . .

Kiko - I waited for you, I was always waiting for you, I was looking for you... I needed you.

Enrique - You hated me. You hate me.

Kiko - Why is it that you could never make of me, of this man here, a real man, a man made of flesh and bones and copper-like skin. . .. a true man, a man that all men could respect, could like, could. . . I. . . Could love?

Enrique - That's it! That's what I mean! Why? Why? Why can't I do it? Why can I never do it?

Kiko - Among the specters you made to people your days, you are the least alive, the least legitimate, the biggest fake of all, the saddest one. . . you yourself. . . A noise unable to ever find his voice.

Enrique - Kiko. . .

Kiko - Among all of us, victims and victimizers, you are the will-o'-the-wisp, the muffled shout, the neutral silence between two shrieks. You have made all those senseless shadows because you cannot love, you cannot hate, you have denied yourself any passion for living. . .

Enrique - I was born to be a witness, I am not an actor. I live only to see. Only to look and to remember.

Kiko - These puppets with a magical voice, these executioners with sweet, bold words, these men made of smoke and water. . . Why is it that they can give life and bring wolves into the world?

Enrique - I am not an actor, I am a witness. . . They live in me forever, my dead.

Kiko - With one day of courage, one lovingly smile. . . With a tender hand in mine, such a small hand then, so weak a hand. . . Everything would have been different. . . I would have been different. . . I could have been another. .

Enrique - My voices will speak forever. My dead will be immortal. They will speak through me to those who are coming, those who are not born yet, those who will make a new, different universe. You kill, you can only kill. . .

I will defeat death!

Kiko - Another child, another man, if only I could have had a glimpse of your world. . . If only you. . . Your martyrs would never deny your world, did you know? They died believing in your world, they could not reject it, they could never. . . But where is this world of yours? Perhaps, if you had given me a taste of tenderness. . .

Enrique - I could not. It was too late. I found out about you too late.

Kiko - It might have been. . . Just with one smile. . . One glance at the right moment. . . I. . . You and me. . . To say and to believe it: I love you. . . To feel, and to know that once I was loved. . . I. . . You could have made everything different. It would have been enough if. . .

Enrique - Enrique, to each his cross!

Kiko - I will be yours, then! A thousand for this damn bastard!

(Shot. Enrique holds his leg. Limps. Exit.)

Kiko - Be careful, my wolves! I want him alive!

(Kicks. Noises. Darkness. Silence.)

(Pause.) (Light.)

Enrique - (Enters.) That story about how I shot myself is inaccurate. He did it. He did this to me. But, how can I tell such a tale? Nobody would believe it. (Lights a cigarette and smokes.)

After that wound, there was no truce in the war of the skin. I decided I should find a place in the world where things could be different. How do they say in these circumstances? I wanted to begin again. I could not change the man or the time, but perhaps if I changed the place. . .

I passed from hand to hand, from roof to basement, from house to cave for a few weeks and then I jumped, without really knowing or understanding it, into freedom. It was a difficult jump. It was grim and hard. We better have a cigarette now, all of us.

(Light. Enrique walks down and chats with several people among the audience till the end of the

Intermission.

North

(Aymara music. A typewriter typing. Penumbra.)
(Pictures of his life and blow-ups of his face, his hands, etc., will "illustrate" Enrique's humankind before been replaced by the first picture of Grand Central Station.)
(Enrique steps on the stage. He walks to the table. He turns around. He stands. He points at himself with the thumb of an open hand.)
Enrique - Ecce homo. Here is the man. 43. Rotten teeth. Bald. Fat. Bawdy. Coarse. Rude, unsophisticated. Shy. Fastidious. Stubborn. Hypochondriac. Chain smoker. Drinker. Sad. Ah! Sad always, without ever knowing the deep causes of this sadness. Childish: a child forever, unable to jump, once and for all, even sideways, into the adult world. A constant reader. Always reading. With one eye. This eye, almost blind after that incident in the cell. Alone. Alone for ever, under the weight of the existential loneliness which marks all bright men in this century. Weak like the sad, the lonely, like all children. Balky as a mule. A broken finger, dead forever. Two trousers, a shirt. Dark glasses, one portable typewriter, one camera under this arm, one pocketknife and one lighter. . . Peculiar trappings to start experiencing freedom and to taste the sweet juices of any democracy.
Loudspeaker - Welcome! Welcome, welcome!
Enrique - (Two steps ahead.) I am free! Free! (Hesitates.) Free? What for? What am I doing here? What's behind that gate? And, above all, after a whole life under the dark night of dictatorships, will I be able to live now under the bright sun of freedom? (Scratches the back of his hand.) Yes. Sí. It must be possible. Freedom is man's natural environment. (Two steps ahead.) Do away, then, with the rags of your old oppressions, man. Be born naked to the world of democracy. . . Be free. Dare to be free! (One step ahead. Open

arms.) Freedom, Ecce homo!

(One step. Out of light. Light fades out. Pause.)

(Light. Enrique enters right. Carries a book. Crowd sounds.)

Enrique - . . .have no business card, just my book. . . (Walks against the crowd. One step ahead, one step back.) I bring the voices of my people. . . The dead, the wounded, the tortured, the blind, the raped. . . There's no justification, besides this frozen scream, for my presence here among you, the free men. I bring a message of anguish and desperation. I bring the eternal howl of the dying, those dying among my people. I bring a call for the men of power in this land so that they make justice and hope possible among my people with one blink of their powerful eyes. I bring the story of their deaths, the daring of their life, the courage of their suffering. . . I bring 40 years of pain, sadness, struggles, heroic deeds, voices. . . Voices. Voices and crying, yelling and howling; the weak rumble of their perennial demand for justice, freedom, democracy, for their right to a piece of bread and to a little hope. . .

I come with my message, my praying, with my dead on my shoulders I come, because I have no other fate. . . I must do my duty, I must justify my new freedom, I must honor the suffering of those who speak through my mouth. I must. . .

(Something hits his arm. He drops the book. He stops.)

Enrique - But. . . Is this worthless too?

Salesman - Walk, man, walk! Don't disrupt us!

Enrique - (Picks up the book.) But. . . I must do this! If I don't, why have I come this far? You must listen to me! You must! They could not come, my friends and comrades, the others could not come; they are dead! You must listen to me! Listen!

Lawyer - No time, man. . . .in a hurry! There's no time!

Secretary - What's more: who cares about the last yelp from the end of the world?

Taxi Driver - We don't know where that place is, who those people are, we don't know what they want, why are they yelling.

Old Woman - Everybody yells, everybody shouts, everybody cries! Why do you come with your crazy voices to shout here, in the heart of this hubbub?

Enrique - You are wrong, señora. It is not I, it's them. They are shouting to be heard here. . . Here, among the powerful men of the world. . . They, my dead, my desaparecidos. . . It is not I. I am but a stuttering messenger, badly chosen by chance. . . Listen to them, please!

José Bonilla - You listen. . . What you doing here?

Enrique - (Puts book under his arm.) I was trying to use my new freedom to justify my life. I am the only one among my people who has come so far with so many voices, so many. . . The voices I bring here. . .

José Bonilla - Where you come from?

Enrique - From the night of the dictatorships. From the South.

José Bonilla - Why you come?

Enrique - Well. . . It's my fate. Lady luck in pink.

José Bonilla - You come what for?

Enrique - I bring my testimony. It is made of foam. . . Black foam, yes. But it is a testimony, anyway. . . It is the only testimony. . . The only. . .

Johnny Paz - What you want here?

Enrique - I, myself?

Johnny Paz - You, you. What you want, here?

Enrique - Well. . . I. . . I wanted. . . I want to learn how to be a man, a human being. I want to forget my old nightmares, those gray dreams that haunt harassed animals. I want to be sure that it is true. . . It is true that I have a right to live. . . It is true that I have a right to my dignity. . . I want to enjoy the satisfaction of going to work every morning without being afraid of the men in uniform, without being afraid of them catching me, ripping me up, killing me as if I was a cockroach. . . I want. . .

María Lopez - What you saying? They kill you like that down there, where you come from?

Enrique - Yes. Sí. They break doors and windows, they push old women, they kick our children. They rape our women, they burn us, they bleed us, they throw us to the dogs. . . While in here. . . In here. . .

José Bonilla - You flee your country because men in uniform could have destroyed you?

Enrique - Right.

Johnny Paz - You flee because there's no safety in the streets? You run away because there's no security in the squares, no policemen on every corner?

Enrique - They are not policemen, they are hounds. . . Hounds, yes. . . They chased me. They haunted me always, to step on me, to crush me, to harm me. . . To annihilate me, to disembowel me or to burn me alive. . .

María Lopez - Here. . . No cops on every corner. . .

Enrique - But there are policemen. . . There is law!

Johnny Paz - It's the law of the streets. You carry twenty bucks in the same pocket so you can be mugged every day. If you are lucky, they won't cut your neck. . . They won't rape you, they won't break your teeth.

Enrique - But. . . But. . . It cannot be!

María Lopez - It is!

Enrique - But. . . What about the law?

Johnny Paz - I'm telling you. It's the law of the streets.

Enrique - And all these people, these people who came as I did?

María Lopez - Somebody has to wash the public toilets, to clean private bathrooms.

Enrique - So I flee to avoid a degenerate in uniform who wanted to kill me there. . .

María Lopez -. . .so that a degenerate without a uniform can kill you here.

Enrique - It can't be so!

María Lopez - It is so!

Enrique - How about freedom?

José Bonilla - You come for your freedom?

Enrique - Well. . . Yes.

María Lopez - Look at your freedom!

(Grand Central Station.Crowd noises intensify and fade away.)

Enrique - (Walks and watches.) All of them. . . Almost all. . . Are fat. . . Fat and healthy. . . Some are so grotesquely fat. . . Not all. . . But everybody looks so well. . . Everybody walks so fast. . . Do they know where are they going? But. . . Wait! What's wrong with this man? (Gesticulates following his words.) This man is dying! So well dressed, so healthy, so. . . He is dying! Stooped on all fours. . . Huddled as pup. . . So elegant. . . He is dying. . .

He is dying squatting as a poisoned cat, blue face and blue hands on the concrete floor and among all these people. . . There must be a million

people in this huge hall. . . This huge temple. . . What is this? What. . . Thing
is this? Among all this. . . This man, slumped and huddled up, on his fours. . .
He is dying without a yelp, without a "Jesus" in his mouth. . . It cannot be, it
cannot be! Is he dying, truly? Let's see. . . (He looks down.) Yes, yes. He is
dying! Come on, man. Come on! It's not so bad, it cannot be so bad. . . Do
something. . . Don't give up. . . Don't fall. . . Don't fall. . . Don't. Put one
foot here. . . That hand here. . . That foot. . . Don't fall! Don't give up! It's
not so bad. . .
(Stands up.)
    My God! He is dying. He is dying! Help, help! This man is dying! His
face is blue. His glance is lost, he breathes like a horse, he is a corpse
already! A dead man who looks like my own dead people, like my very own
dead. . . It cannot be! Help! No, it's not true: he is pretending, it's a trick, all
this is a false game. Nobody can die like this, so alone, alone in a desert,
while thousands and thousands go passing by in a hurry. . . How many are
passing by? How many are coming and going? Millions!
    You cannot die like this! You cannot die like my dead die up there, in
our frozen desert. . . Don't die. Are you listening? Don't die! Don't die, I say!
You cannot die like this, among so many people. . . Listen to me!
Pablo Curcio - What you doing?
Enrique - This man is dying! We must help him! I must help him! Help!
Pablo Curcio - Let him be.
Enrique - Let him. . . But, what are you saying? Let him be! I cannot!
Pablo Curcio - Let him be!
Enrique - But. . . No!
Pablo Curcio - Let him be, I say! If you touch him and he dies, you will
have to be a witness later. You will have to say what you saw, what you
knew, where were you, who are you. You must go to the judges. . .
Enrique - Judges? Which judges? Why judges? I did nothing!
Mario Arauco - Who will believe you? It's the law!
Enrique - The law?
Voices - The law of the streets!
Enrique - (Hesitates. Unwillingly, he goes away. Two steps. Looks back.)
You mean to say that he will die right there, he will die with two moans, and

nobody will give him a hand?

Mario Arauco - They will come later. To pick him up. . .

Enrique - Why? Why must this be so? It cannot be so. We must help him!

Ursula Romero -. . .or rob him, perhaps?

Enrique - (Shocked.) Rob him? Rob him, me? But, but, but! (Gagged.)

Roberto Sacoto - It was your fang in his chest?

Enrique - What's a fang?

Gustavo Sotelo - You cut him with your knife!

Enrique - No. . . No! What are you saying? You are crazy! What are you saying! I wanted to help him, I only wanted to help him! The poor man was dying. . . And I. . .

Roberto Sacoto - You were there, there with your knife in your hand, you murderer! Your long arm with your killing knife!

Enrique - No! (One step back. He backs up fast.) No! I did nothing! I don't have a knife! I never had a knife! I did nothing! I did nothing! Nothing!

Voices - Pickpocket! Killer!

Enrique - I did nothing! I only wanted to help him! He was dying!

José Bonilla - It's your word against ours!

Enrique - (Huddles up, in fright.) I did nothing! I am innocent! I did nothing!

Juan Rodriguez - Besides, your papers? Your driving license?

María Lopez - Driver's license? Who are you?

Enrique - I have no papers yet. . . I. . .

Voices - You are nobody! You are nothing! Murderer! Robber!

Enrique - You are crazy! I only wanted to help him! What's wrong with you? You look like rabid dogs!

Johnny Perez - What you say? Can't understand you!

Voices - We don't understand! We can't understand!

Enrique - Oh, so you don't understand me, either?

Voices - What's he saying? What's he talking about? What's he shrieking about?

Enrique - They want a translator! Who can translate, around here? Who translates? We need a translator!

(Turns around. Exits.)

(Fade Off. Pause. Fade on.)

THE WORK PLACE

(General picture of a huge hall with many computer cubicles.)
Partial pictures taken from this first picture will be used later as blow-ups to
illustrate each character when it talks, creating in this way a "persona" for
each voice. These blow-ups will show faces, hands, any particular trait or
gesture that adds to each character.)
(Light.)
(Enrique with men and women. White shirt. Blue Tie. Gray pants. Empty
stare. They move like puppets.)
Jorge - I translate.
Enrique - We translate here.
Carlos - Each man writes eleven thousand words a day.
Luis - In a beautiful word processor. Clean, accurate, infallible.
Abel - Infallible.
Mario - Infallible Cyclops of the green eye.
Felix - The processor, in Dallas, is insatiable.
Patricia - Insatiable.
Alberto - Infallible, insatiable Cyclops of the green eye.
Enrique - Like the miners in my town, we work three shifts a day.
Abel - 24 hours a day.
Felix - Some days, we work 26 hours a day.
Patricia - Or thirty.
Mario - Eleven thousand words a day. Each day, each man.
Gustavo - Two thousand men.
Carlos - 22 million, 636 thousand, 456 words every day.
Luis - It is an insatiable computer. It's in Dallas.
Alberto - Here, we process words.
Enrique - I translate. I used to think, not long ago. I often thought nonsense
but, still, I used to think. Now, I translate. I used to be a journalist. Now, I am
a puppet. A puppet that makes an endless string of words like sausages. A
puppet who forgets everything he translates as soon as he translates anything.

Abel - It is not good to remember whatever you translate. Not good for your own mind. It's called mental hygiene.

Luis - It is not good for anybody else, because one could remember what one translates, and one could talk about it later.

Mario - Here, we care for quantity.

Patricia - Quality is nonsense.

Germán - Here we process documents by the millions. . . Millions and millions. . . Thousands of papers every minute. . . As if these were papers. . . Words are forever swimming in the machine's infallible memory. . . We never see a paper. . .

Luis - Hundreds of millions. . .

Felix -. . .billions and trillions. . .

Carlos - Propaganda, advertising, handbooks, agreements, contracts, pacts, treatises, letters to your grandma, love letters, reports, stories, notes, memos, analyses, studies, for your eyes only, narrations, short stories, true stories, porno stories, cooking recipes. . .

Germán - Everything goes: receipts, speeches, statements, lawsuits, divorces, commentaries, appeals, demands, novels, news, news, news, dollars, dollars, dollars, dollars. . . (Fade off).

Enrique - Eleven thousand words every day, or every night, and one is free. Free to enjoy the cool autumn days. . . But, when one goes out, it's dark already. One never sees the day.

Felix - Working by night, one sleeps by day.

Mario - Processing by day, one comes out to night.

Patricia - One never sees day.

Abel - This summer was very hot, they say.

Jorge - This winter we had no snow, they say. Just rain.

Luis - We process words.

Germán - What hurts. . . What really hurts, is not our soul.

Mario - It's our buttocks.

Felix - To work and be seated like this, word processing and data processing, is a brutal job.

Alberto - People don't know about this, but this word processing job, this processing of any data, by hand or by machine, is a grueling job, a killer, a vicious task.

Abel - One sits here for eight hours, and then one cannot move his legs.

Mario - One has cramps in his legs.

Patricia - One eats next to these machines. One has breakfast and lunch and dinner next to this green eye.

Felix - One man died next to this thing, they say.

Jorge - Don't think. . . No need to think. . . Everything is automatic.

Germán - Efficiency, we call it.

Luis - This hall is huge and cold because that's what the machines demand.

Alberto - Windows are never opened for fresh air and sunny light because that's what the machines need.

Jorge - There's silence on Floor 67. Always silence. Machines need silence.

Felix - Silence, cold and shadows: the machine's graves.

Carlos - No! Our graves.

Germán - Machines don't make mistakes. They don't get sick. They know everything there is to be known. They never forget anything. They don't go to strike.

Luis - Machines laugh at us. They break our backs.

Carlos - They burn our eyes.

Jorge - They dry our brains.

Felix - We are three hundred here, and all of us have mole eyes.

Abel - A broken back.

Mario - Thick glasses, like bottle bottoms, on our eyes.

Patricia - Our faces are green.

Luis - We never see the sun.

Felix - We never walk. We spend our whole life seated in these nice chairs.

Roberto - Our bellies don't work anymore. We get fat like pigs.

Jorge - Our minds are burnt when we get to the street. We don't want to do anything by then. Just sleep. . .

Alberto - We don't sleep well; therefore, we drink.

Felix - Some need pills to sleep.

Germán - Machines are beautiful, tireless, perfect.

Luis - We are not; we degenerate each day, we deform ourselves. We are shadows of men. . .

Patricia - What comes first, the egg or the hen?

Enrique - It's not so bad, it's not so hard. . . Especially if we compare it with the mines in my valley, the canneries in my plains, everyday hunger in my country. . . There's peace here.

Germán - Pain in our buttocks. Bellies that don't work. One smells like a corpse. . .

Enrique - One is not happy. How can one be happy if he was hoping for freedom and there's nothing for him but a pain in the buttocks?

Abel - At the end of the day, one walks down to the subway. One is free.

(Light fades off. Darkness.)

THE SUBWAY STATION

(General picture of a subway station in Manhattan.)

(Partial pictures taken from this first picture will be used later as blow-ups to illustrate each character when it talks, creating a "persona" for each voice. These blow-ups will show faces, hands, any particular trait or gesture that adds to each character.)

(Lights fade on.)

(Subway noises. Enrique enters. Winter cloths. Two steps. The subway station. A newsstand.)

Felipe Alcón - Welcome. What have you done?

Enrique - Thank you. What do you mean?

Dr. Martínez - These are the nerves of the capital of the world. Here, everything is possible.

José del Granado - This is the monument to the Man of the Galaxies. All his work, his dreams, his thoughts, his nightmares, his poems, his songs, his terrors. . . All are here.

Luisa Tovar - One can see, touch, smell, taste and feel everything, here. One chews and smokes the undying works of the Galactic Man.

Echo - With money.

Luisa Tovar - This is the head of the world.

Casildo Herrera - The belly of the universe.

Luis Paniagua - You find everything here.

Juan "Six Fingers" - Everything.

Federico Troche - Everything. . . And more!

Felipe Alcón - Here, man is free.

Ricardo Gomez - Free. To do whatever he wants. Whatever he may demand, need, steal, conquer, control, destroy, invent, create, synthesize.

Santiago Najar - Free to believe or create.

Echo - With money.

Alex Ruiz - Here, and only here, everything is possible.

Juan Franco - Today a bum, tomorrow the king of the world. . .

Echo - With money.

Robertson Gamboa - Cars, TV sets, copy machines, shirts, t-shirts, shoes, socks, pipes, bathtubs, hi-fi's, music boxes, washing machines, drying machines, toasters, ironing machines, roasters, skids, balls, watches and clocks, videos, computers, knives, guns, machine guns. Bombs, canons, howitzers, hot-dogs, airplanes, bottles, stamps, tables, paintings, plants, dogs, cats, pigs, canaries, camels, elephants, flies, ice creams. . . (fade away).

Enrique - My hopes and dreams?

Echo - With money.

Enrique - With money?

Rigoberto Díaz - Yes, with money. Make your money, man!

Enrique - How?

Rigoberto Díaz - No matter how!

Eva Gonzalez - There's a price for everything. . .

Juan Franco - . . .for everybody. . .

Alex Ruiz - Because everybody and everything can be sold. . .

Santiago Najar - Every man can be sold. . .

Eva Gonzalez - Man and woman, mind you.

Darío Perez - Sell the red dream of the white powder!

Enrique - We have a lot of that. . . 40 thousand tons every year.

Darío Perez - 40 thousand tons!

Enrique - But it's a crime.

Felix Coronado - Nothing is a crime! Poverty is the only crime.

Ronald Villarroel - Misery is the only crime.

Lucinda Real - The only sin: an empty pocket!

Felix Coronado - Sell!

Lucinda Real - Buy!

Darío Perez - What was a crime yesterday will be law tomorrow. . .

Lucinda Real - If somebody needs the magic powder, somebody has to provide it.

Rigoberto Díaz - If somebody buys, somebody can sell.

Ramiro Lopera - Everything has a price.

Eva Gonzalez - Everybody.

Juan Franco - The magic touch.

Alex Ruiz - Sell and buy.

Voices - And freedom!

Juan "Six Fingers" - What's more. . . That's not a crime, its a job.

El Michi - Sell it! Buy it! Use it! It's crack time!

Juan Franco - Enjoy anal sex. . .

Enrique - I'm sorry, sir. I can't do it.

Lucero Peralta - Fool! Night will be your friend. . .

Juan Franco - It's a simple choice: if you want money. . .

Enrique - Please, don't say more. . .

Juan "Six Fingers" - You get money. . . Or you get a job.

El Michi - Choose, you are free!

Enrique - I better go home.

El Michi - Can you turn your back to all this?

Lucero Peralta - Night in the city is happiness for the urban animal.

Dr. Martínez - And this is the capital of the world!

Enrique - With money.

Echo - With money.

Enrique - And I have no money.

Dr. Martínez - Lady Luck goes with daring gents!

Enrique - I am not a criminal!

Lucero Peralta - Nobody is innocent any more.

José del Granado - Innocent, perhaps not. . . But free!

Luisa Tovar - Free by definition.

Casildo Herrera - By law.

Federico Troche - Here, only the poor are to be blamed for their poverty.

Felipe Alcón - That's why you see so few poor people. Poor people like you, like the old ladies with brown paper bags.

Ricardo Gomez - If I am poor today, it's because I never used my freedom to make money.

Santiago Najar - Freedom without this other face, the face of failure, would not be true freedom.

Alex Ruiz - Some use their freedom to conquer success and money. . .

Juan Franco - Some use their freedom to slowly die in failure and poverty.

Robertson Gamboa - Failure and poverty are sisters, from the South.

Ramiro Lopera - Success and wealth are brothers, from the North.

Rigoberto Díaz - If one uses his freedom to fail, one can blame nobody for his poverty.

Eva Gonzalez - One cannot rebel against anybody.

Alex Ruiz - One is the only forger of his fate. One, alone. Alone.

Darío Roncal - One. One makes himself or destroys himself. Alone.

Felix Coronado - Mass man. . . Faceless, shadowless, voiceless man. . .

Ronald Villarroel - This mass man struggles and fights and conquers the universe. . .

Roque Arias - He forges himself!

Santiago Najar - Galactic Man! Not just a universal man; Galactic Man!

Darío Roncal - The Master of the Universe!

Luis Paniagua - The father of the clone!

Rigoberto Díaz - The Magellan of the Milky Way!

Enrique - But if his freedom is no more than traveling in this cage on wheels. . .

Federico Troche - If this is the only freedom he dared to conquer, it suits him.

Ricardo Gomez - He's the only one to blame. . .

Juan Franco - Other people never ever come down here. . . They do not know the subway. . .

Alex Ruiz - Each step takes them to success, wealth, power, freedom's harvest.

Felix Coronado - Each one is made by his own toil under the sun of freedom.

Enrique - But down here they seem to be paying a weighty debt, an eternal debt. . . They seem to be suffering too long a sentence, a heavy and constant punishment.

Casildo Herrera - Failure is a crime.

José del Granado - Poverty is a sin.

Lucinda Real - The worst crime. The scourge of the world.

María Tovar - The only true crime!

Ramiro Lopera - Poverty is catchy. It stains everything. It soiles everybody. It corrodes souls, and faces and bodies.

Federico Troche - It corrodes and corrupts.

Alex Ruiz - It brutalizes. It animalizes. It maddens, right?

Santiago Najar - It prostitutes. It makes murderers and fanatics.

Lucero Peralta - It pushes the father against his son, the mother against her daughter. . . Old people starve and die crazy and alone.

 Ramiro Lopera - The law against poverty is so wise and pure, it was never written.

Darío Roncal - No need to write it.

Felix Coronado - Not for men; not for nations.

Santiago Najar - But when one man travels in the subway with his poverty on his back, it catches everybody else.

Luisa Tovar - Poverty is like bane.

Ricardo Gomez - It shows up anywhere, and one cannot anticipate it. It appears wherever one least expects it. In whatever strait. In any neighborhood which was prospering just yesterday.

Darío Roncal - In a flash, it rules men, women, homes, houses, gardens, roofs and baby cradles; its a loathsome patina.

Alex Ruiz - It ties hands. It drowns human imagination, it blinds one's vision.

Dr. Martínez - It kills one's dreams.

Ramiro Lopera - The man who brings poverty to his neighborhood is a criminal.

Santiago Najar - Man or woman, mind you..

José del Granado - Man or woman. . .. The worst criminal of all.

Robertson Gamboa - And his punishment is as horrible as his terrible crime.

Darío Roncal - The only true crime in the world!

Girl - Dignity can live together with poverty, right?

Ricardo Gomez - Bull. Lies. Humbug. . .

Roque Arias - Poverty kills all dignity.

Girl - Poor people don't make poverty. . . Nobody wants to be poor; don't blame them for their poverty.

Luisa Tovar - Here, the poor are guilty of their poverty.

Darío Roncal - We are all born equal. We all have opportunities to make money while we are free.

Dr. Martínez - And we are free since we are born till we die.

Felix Coronado - Some make money under the shield of the law, and their money talks.

Robertson Gamboa - Some make money against the shield of the law, and their money talks.

Felix Coronado - When money talks, laws change.

Robertson Gamboa - Yesterday, Prohibition; tomorrow, addiction!

Ricardo Gomez - Whoever uses his freedom with daring sagacity makes money.

José del Granado - A man is sentenced to make money in this game.

María Tovar - A man or a woman, mind you. . .

Dr. Martínez - One cannot make anything else. Unless one lies on the sidewalk waiting for death.

Robertson Gamboa - But then, everybody else throws money on him.

María Tovar - Him or her, mind you. . .

Felix Coronado - Yeah, until she is buried in money.

Darío Roncal - That might have been long ago. . .

Roque Arias - Freedom blesses its children and provides them with a vision of human power.

José del Granado - Free, and only free, is man a true man.

María Tovar - Man or. . .

José del Granado - Oh, shut up, will you?

Ramiro Lopera - Free, man holds the law in his left hand and the future in his right hand.

Robertson Gamboa - Each man is free and enjoys the fruits of his freedom.

Darío Roncal - Or suffers because of the fruits of his freedom.

Luisa Tovar - Men choose their fate. They forge it. They make it step by step.

Enrique - Men, perhaps. . . But I don't see men in the subway. I only see apes.

Ricardo Gomez - Apes?

Felix Coronado - Apes!

José del Granado - Apes, he says!

Ricardo Gomez - Apes?

Enrique - Yes, apes! Apes! Hairy apes and naked apes. Yellow apes, gray apes, bronze apes and mahogany apes. . . Apes made of ivory, copper or coal.

Robertson Gamboa - Apes? Apes. Apes!

Enrique - Deformed apes, mute, small, giant, strong, effeminate, rude, thin, fat, anguished, afraid. . . But apes. . . Apes!

Robertson Gamboa - Apes!

Enrique - Apes, yes. Apes!

José del Granado - He says, apes! Apes, he says.

Enrique - Apes.

Ramiro Lopera - Nobody can call us apes.

Roque Arias - It's a crime.

Luis Tovar - To call us apes is to break the law; a law conquered with blood.

Casildo Herrera - The law is clear: nobody will suffer injustice, abuses, exploitation because of his skin, his religion, his race or his ideas.

María Tovar - His or her ideas, mind you. . .

Dr. Martínez - Nobody is different. We are all equal.

Darío Roncal - By law.

Robertson Gamboa - By law, nobody is an ape, down here. We are all human beings. We are all entitled to be considered and respected. The law deals the same chips to everybody, and we all are equal down here.

Rigoberto Díaz - Nobody is an ape because nobody wants to be an ape.

Casildo Herrera - We are all men of the galaxies!

Enrique - But these are apes, I am telling you! These are apes. Look at their bodies. Look at their faces. Watch their gestures. Look at their clothes. Listen to them: they cannot talk! They never talk. They scream. They yell. They bark like chimps in their cages on wheels.

José del Granado - Apes! Nobody can call us apes!

Enrique - They are apes!

José del Granado - It's the law!

Enrique - The subway is a sewer! A long, dark sewer!

Dr. Martínez - A sewer!

Darío Roncal - A sewer, he says!

Enrique - A sewer, yes! They have a sewer for industrial refuse, they make another for excrement and trash. They make one sewer for chemical refuse, and another yet for us, we, the human refuse, for these poor criminals, these poor and criminal traveling in our own sewer, the midnight subway!

Robertson Gamboa - You travel in the subway!

Enrique - Yes. That's what freedom has done to me, I travel in my assigned sewer.

Ricardo Gomez - But you are free! You can choose!

Enrique - I can choose what I can pay. This sewer is my world, and I have none other. . . To work, I must take the subway. To see my children again, I must take the subway. The subway is my day to day cage, it is my cell every night. It's my life, this sewer! It's my only sky, the only memory of the sun that I have. . . This is my only garden, and it stinks!

Luisa Tovar - You don't understand freedom!

Enrique - Yes, I do: instead of smiling at me, it has shown me its buttocks. And freedom also has a pain in her buttocks.

Dr. Martínez - Understand, you are free! Understand, you can choose!

Enrique - I understand; I am free. I can choose between these apes and their law of the knives. . . Or the cells and torture from the long knives I have fled.

Felix Coronado - But you are blind. You cannot understand freedom!

Enrique - This is my freedom: I chose this sewer because, if I am lucky, I won't be killed before my children can get a job. . . And by then, if they kill me, so what?

Ricardo Gomez - What you saying? What you saying?

Enrique - My chest aches. I am so tired that I must go home. (To the audience, with interest.) We are very close here. We live happily. In a humble place, perhaps, but we are happy here, my family and me. Here comes my

train. (Turns around.)
(Darkness.)

THE SUBWAY

(General picture of a subway car.)
(Partial pictures taken from this first picture will be used later as blow-ups to illustrate each character when it talks, creating in this way a "persona" for each voice. These blow-ups will show faces, hands, any particular trait or gesture that adds to each character.)
(Under a light beam, Enrique hangs from his right arm, holding a strap. His body follows the car's stops and departures. He looks like a big piece of meat hanging in a slaughterhouse. He switches his arm from time to time. Shifts from one leg to the other, searching for a comfortable position. He travels alone, and spies this way and that from time to time. He looks at the ceiling, he eats his nails, he plays with his nose, etc. Enrique does not "live" this scene; he *dreams* it in the noise and clangor of the subway, a clangor that grows and decreases as a background. He'll talk only once, at the very end of this scene.)
Fat Man - After the first six hundred nights in the subway, the same route and at the same time, many try some reading in the train.
Thin Man in Black - That's a mistake, because one can learn a thousand things, a thousand ideas and thousand important political theories in the train. I never read in the subway. I look, see, and learn.
Man with Violin Case - History is amassed with the masses of the train.
Hunk - The subway is freedom's dirty face.
Dandy - The face of freedom as mother of poverty.
Enrique - (Voice off.) Back in my country, I know who to blame for my poverty: my government. I am entitled to rebellion in my country because I am poor. I am poor because I am not free. The day I am free, I will never again be poor. That's why I live.
Cowboy - The street and the subway are freedom's children. It is here where a nameless wisdom chooses between the strong and the weak.
Construction Worker - It is here where the weak are trounced until they

perish.

Woman with Radio Box - Nobody kills them; they just die.

Woman in Furs - They die alone; they cannot blame anybody for their death.

Man with Books - They blame themselves, yes. It's just fair.

Man with Beard - Their weakness punishes them, and they die as any other culprit, but they need no executioner.

Man with Flowers - They die. That's all.

Fat Prostitute - Like flowers in winter.

Man with Violin Case - Like birds in a drought.

Jogger - Like an ant under your thumb.

Old Queen - They go crazy. They grow ugly cancers, dirty tumors and strange manges in their body and their soul. But nobody kills them. They die.

Woman in Night Gown - They die, and some kill before they die.

Homeless Lady - So what? We are all criminals, because we all are poor. . . Look at their faces. . . Look at the subway faces of the night. . .

Asian Man - We are all shadows of hell!

Preacher with old Bible - But free.

Priest with Eye Patch - Free.

Safari Guide - Free.

Asian Man - These faces. . . These faces. . . We all lack a bit of sunlight. We have these green faces. . . These yellow pale faces, faces of corpses, already, walking corpses. . .

Nun with painted Face - Yep, we are not pretty. We all suffer from some peculiar tics, some little spring badly sprung. . . And we make faces we don't want to make.

Man with Books - Faces. Faces like this, like this or like this.

Body Builder - Look at the eyes. There's a tic for each eye.

Woman in Night Gown - Look the eyes' tic. How loathsome!

Priest with Eye Patch - Oh, their glances! All glances get lost in a void.

Homeless Lady - The price of each straight glance in the midnight subway is a knife in the guts, a kick in the balls, a broken bottle used to gorge an eye, a karate kick in the neck.

Thin Man in Black - Only thieves look straight into the eyes of their victims, or addicts into the night.

Old Queen - That's why you must learn fast. Listen, now:

Safari Guide - Never turn your back to anybody; never look into anybody's eyes.

Hunk - Remember, you're risking your life!

Body Builder - Never talk to strangers. Always have twenty bucks for the man with his brain in a cloud that plays with a knife.

Woman with Radio Box - We the humble, those of us who cannot kill, we look at the floor like this, like this, or like this. . .

Thin Man in Black - We look at the ceiling like this, like this and this. . . An empty, lightless glance. . .

Fat Prostitute - Or we don't look at all. We feign nightmares or we close our eyes like this, a very dangerous exercise, indeed.

Fat Man - (Yells.) Announcing: The Nose Festival!

Hunk - Noses. . . Look at the noses. . . Noses frown and hide behind gloves and fingers like this, get covered by handkerchiefs this way, or disappear behind a newspaper like this. . .

Thin Man in Black - Noses also help to hide behind green glasses, black glasses, thick glasses or funny glasses.

Asian Man - Noses have their own tics too: some nose tics are like this, some are like this, but most are like this, this or this. One seldom seen nose tic goes like this: tic!

Cowboy -The mouths in the subway!

Man with Beard - Mouths get funny too! Often, just to breathe. . . Also, to yawn. Some mouths are always open, like this, open forever.

Woman with Radio Box - Mouths find relief by chewing, licking or lapping.

Preacher with Old Bible - Gum, tobacco, pills, tablets.

Dandy - Mouths are deep tunnels at five o'clock, when most passengers sleep.

Man with Violin Case - At five, mouths open like this, this, this and like this. Some are opened like this. A few look like this and this.

Nun with Painted Face - These faces belong to the subway. Nobody would make such faces in his home.

Jogger - Not at Sunday church. Nobody. Unless he's nuts.

Little Old Lady - But in the subway, madness is mental health.

Man with Flowers - And sanity is madness.

Little Old Lady - Mad people don't shock anybody in the subway.

Enrique - (Voice. Off.) The sewer's culture.

Fat Man - Look at these bodies!

Woman in Furs - Oh, our bodies! This is a different race. We are mutants. Nothing to do with the primeval talking ape.

Priest with Eye Patch - Every excess leads to every malformation.

Man with Beard - In winter, we are all bears with plastic and cotton hides.

Boy in Heavy Overcoat - In summer, we show our own skin, naked.

Midget with Cigar - Almost.

Construction Worker - So that all kinds of fat, hair, excrescences, tattoos and scars are exhibited as medals.

Cowboy - We see overgrown heads on mini-skeletons.

Man with Violin Case - Shrunken jibaro heads on fat bubbles.

Homeless Lady - There's no human beauty. A beautiful human being in the subway is like a flower in winter.

Safari Guide - A miracle, an inconceivable accident. . .

Boy in Heavy Overcoat - I saw two beautiful women once. Once in the last thirteen years.

Construction Worker - We mutants are not only children of excess, abuse and chance.

Nun with Painted Face - We are walking portraits of every vice and every laceration inflicted by the seven capital sins to the human body, God's main temple.

Safari Guide - Gluttony, a massive sport, parades its living monuments down here.

Man with Books - Monumental monuments!

Hunk - Alcohol destroys faces, creates swollen bellies.

Woman in Night Gown - And the opposite sins. . . To look thin, women do as Roman emperors once did: anorexia; they throw up thrice a day and live on strange mixtures; they are starving serpents. . . Dreadful witches. . .

Man with Violin Case - Look at the sporting types: scarecrows with arms like elm stalks.

Woman in Furs - We often see some human hippos!

Man with Flowers - Shaved heads on huge fat ladies.

Old Queen - And huge fat teats hanging from talking wire frames.

Construction Worker - Old hermaphrodites with painted faces purring like wild cats.

Preacher with Old Bible - Strongmen staring at the void who cry like little babies.

Fat Man - Virginal angels brandishing their four-feet penises.

Jogger - Children stomp in the subway hunting for little old ladies to kill a la Kung Fu. . .

Safari Guide - Police dogs look at men with indifference, at women with anguish, at young human bodies with sexual hunger.

Boy in Heavy Overcoat - These trains are like crazy godlike ejaculations against every star of this universe in a mad dance, a crazy game of chance. . .

Midget with Cigar - There is, nevertheless, an unavoidable fact: we are all monsters in the subway.

Fat Man - Our voices?

Woman with Radio Box - Our voices? We have no voices! Only machines which crackle and creak and whistle and howl and kill our voices.

Thin Man in Black - If one travels alone. . . One always travels alone in the subway. Always. One does not need to talk.

Jogger - If two travel together, both travel alone, really, because nobody can talk. One must yell, howl against this perennial clangor, this endless thunder made of tin cans, brakes, the sighs and the roaring of the metal dragon that eats and regurgitates us.

Homeless Lady - Nobody talks here. If one hollers, it's the shriek of the primordial beast. One barks or roars.

Nun with Painted Face - One howls or dies.

Thin Man in Black - One shouts: "Help! Gaaaaaaaah! (Barks) Gruff, gruff, gruff!"

Woman with Radio Box - That's all. A storm made of metal thundering.

Midget with Cigar - How about love, Jock?

Fat Man - Love is copulae, Jack.

Woman with Radio Box - Love is impossible, down here.

Thin Man in Black - Because love is impossible and it's copulae, these lovers show off their public passion only to grow a tacit envy among everybody else. . .

Man with Beard - They go both welded, nine years old or ninety, male and female, male and male, female, male and female, or female, female and female, who cares what they are? They twist, they drivel, they spoon without modesty, they writhe and squirm and ignore everything else, they are grotesque imitations of dogs in heat.

Hunk - Oh, love in the subway! It harms your eyes, it perverts your soul, it debases all of us, all of us. . .

Fat Man - Sick, desperate love made of pretended copulae against loneliness. . .

Boy in Heavy Overcoat - The eyes, the eyes!

Body Builder - These eyes are mirrors of murdered souls, because to have a soul in the subway is an unbearable flaw.

Priest with Eye Patch - The subway eyes murdered innocence a thousand years ago.

Homeless Lady - These eyes liquefy, go empty, get turned off, dry away.

Dandy - These are fish eyes, eyes made of old, cracked glass.

Cowboy - Wise as old vices and sins. Nothing can shock these eyes, nothing can move them, nothing can enliven them.

Man with Beard - These eyes have chosen blindness. The sun scares them because they never see the sun. They search for shadows because in shadows they survive, they avoid other glances. . .

Midget with Cigar - Subway eyes hide behind strange glasses of electric colors, look for cover behind newspapers and magazines, go half closed because there's no worse haunting than constant terror. . .

Man with Flowers - The subway eyes are like tombstones, the ultimate doors closed by the big void. . .

Asian Man - (Yells.) What about clothing?!

Preacher with Old Bible - Rags. We all wear rags. We are all rags. New rags and old rags. Nothing but rags.

Hunk - Filth here is different. It throbs and lives and stains everything. It's a jelly that seems to hang from our eyelids. Neon-made filth.

Little Old Lady - Our clothes are mirrors of our minds, our senseless, absurd, desperate minds.

Man with Violin Case - These clothes portray our thinking, or what's left of it after years and years of thunder and noise, this noise that comes from everywhere, this constant thunder, this monstrous voice of the subway and its mother, the city. . .

Fat Prostitute - If silence was brought to these stinky tunnels, we would run away like crazy cockroaches.

Dandy - This train is a blind Cyclops that runs through an eternal night in the bottom of the earth. . .

Woman with Radio Box - Inside this fast worm, this worm in rags, painted, scratched, tainted and signed by our urine, our excrement and our graffiti, we go from nowhere to nowhere. . . We, the new barbarians of the technological century.

Safari Guide - Flashing our rags like uniforms, wearing and showing off the rags of our hearts and minds like medals. . . In our nakedness and our hides the rags of our souls. . .

Homeless Lady - The subway rags are the spirit, the picture and the breathe of the rags we have carved in the human soul.

Thin Man in Black - (Preaching.) Immense punishment, your eyes. . . Punishment like none, your ears. . . Heavy pain, this, in your chest, having to travel four times a day, three hours each time, shoulder to shoulder, head to head, elbow to elbow, race to race, back to back and face to face, like animals to the slaughterhouse. . .

Man with Violin Case - Day in and day out, month in and month out, every year, every life, every man and every woman. . .

Enrique - Democracy, alive and strong, inside a tuna can.

Fat Man - A mute desperation, in which we cannot yell, we cannot cry or mourn, because nobody listens. Nobody listens, ever!

Safari Guide - Unless we kill.

Priest with Eye Patch - Amok!

Hunk - Amok.

Woman with Radio Box - When a spring in one's head gets broken and you keep shotguns and Saturday Night Specials in each closet. . .

Woman in Furs - Amok!

Jogger - When you cry for justice, but you are but smoke and glass, and nobody can see you or listen to you. . .

Woman with Radio Box - Amok.

Asian Man - When you smoke one last joint, the sourest one, and one keeps two knives in the kitchen, dark and stinky. . .

Hunk - Amok.

Woman with Radio Box - When baby gets sick, and cannot sleep and baby cries and cries and cries. . .

Man with Violin Case - Amok.

Priest with Eye Patch - When its hot and its dark and the night is heavy. . . (Shriek.)

Little Old Lady - Amok.

Fat Man - Time has come. Time to pay your debts and collect your credits, time to clean the world with blood. . .

Enrique - (Looking to far left.) Excuse me. That's the subway, or so they say. I must get off here. This is my neighborhood. Have a good day. (Exits. Dark.)

THE NEIGHBORHOOD

(General picture of a Queens street.)

(Partial pictures taken from this first picture will be used later as blow-ups to illustrate each character when it talks, creating in this way a "persona" for each voice. These blow-ups will show faces, hands, or any particular trait or gesture that adds to each character.)

Enrique - (Standing, hands in pockets. Looking right.) I am learning Korean. My neighbor is my teacher. We all live in a huge refugee camp. Of course, nobody calls it a camp. But it is a refugee camp. This is Elmhurst.

Lucho Campos - We are the refugees of this century's official wars.

Lucho Vidal - Of the last 45 years' unofficial wars.

Prof. Anaya - Wars written about in history books and wars just mentioned in passing on magazines, newspapers and TV news. The poppy wars, the coca wars. The banana wars, the heroin wars. . . The tin war and the copper war. . . The toilet-paper wars. . .

Dr. Ferrufino - We are all alien, look around: Chinese, Vietnamese, Pakistanis, Indostanis, Haitians, Colombians, Koreans, Congolese. . .

Ms. Ferrufino - Guyanese, Tibetans, Mexicans, Brasilians, Argentines, Uruguayans, Paraguayans, Bolivians, Peruvians, Ecuadorians. Quechuas and Aymaras, Araucanians and Fueguinos.

Juan Calderón - Salvadorans, who came long ago. Guatemalans, Hondurans, Costaricans.

Pedro Ocampo - Cubans, of course. They have their own Cuba here. Chileans, too. People who fled every battleground. . .

Carlos Teruel - We are all, of course, foreigners.

Rita Ruibal - We also have some locals.

Jorge Luiz - Locals who are now foreigners among so many foreigners.

Orfeo Angeluz - They are foreigners who suffer most because their town has turned into a refugee camp.

Ricardo Tapia - All these are little towns; towns built side by side, shoulder to shoulder, each one with its own city hall, its own community home, its police station, its fire station, its hospital, pharmacy, movie house, porno saloon and its nice bar.

Dr. Bernal - Locals suffer more than anybody else. Elder locals, in particular, suffer because they have seen with their own eyes how their little towns have become a pandemonium.

Rex Rodo - They step out often, clean as a whistle, and they stand up on any corner, open mouthed and shocked, when they find themselves in a Hong Kong street. . .

Luis Bocangel - A Caracas corner, a Río slum, a Bogotá street or a Tijuana eatinghouse. . .

Eloy Blasco - Not to mention Islamabad, New Dehli, Buenos Aires and Port au Prince.

Marina Delgado - We all share one trait: we all love freedom.

Blas Ramirez - We love freedom more than many other people, and we have left everything behind for our love of freedom.

Voices - We are exiled.

Voices - We are expatriated.

Marina Delgado - Expatriates belong to one of two huge families.

Sandro Careaga - Those who fled from dictatorships, torture and killing, which may be quite different. . . And those who fled hunger and misery, which are always the same.

Jaime Perez - Political refugees flee from totalitarian regimes, and we are legitimate. Some of us.

Hernán Pereira - Economic refugees flee from hunger and poverty. We have been declared lawless. Illegal.

Felipe Ostos - Illegals must learn, therefore, that it is not difficult to legalize their hunger and poverty.

Hermes Cortéz - It only takes some killing: to kill a dictator's agent and then, but only then, to flee.

Felipe Ostos - Caution: never kill the dictator himself.

Juan Ruiz - Because then you will never be a refugee.

Jaime Perez - You will be a killer VIP.

Rex Rodo - Even so, nothing can help a refugee better than having killed somebody. Or having tried to kill somebody.

Adalberto Pando - To starve is never a brave act.

Jesus Ruiz - To starve is stupid.

Pedro Triana - To flee while killing or to kill while fleeing is always a brave act.

Jack Mamani - When you kill the right killer, it is even a moral act.

Luis Tirado - Ergo: a refugee must be a criminal to be legitimate.

Enrique - Such is life. Excuse me. I live here.

(Turns around and exits.)

(Lights fade off.) (Pause.)

(Lights fade on.)

THE APARTMENT

(Family picture. Father, mother, Vera, 8; Cecilia, 12; Alejo, 11.)

(Partial pictures taken from this first picture will be used later as blow-ups to illustrate each character when it talks, creating in this way a "persona" for each voice. These blow-ups will show faces, hands, or any particular trait or gesture that adds to each character.)

(Light.)

Enrique - (Enters. Green Shirt.) Good morning!

Yolanda - I can see a special charm in here, Enrique. It is a call this place makes, a challenge, an invitation.

Voice - You who are nothing, you who are nobody, you who have nothing, who have been rejected by your own, who have been stalked, tortured, burnt, shot at, trounced, robbed, loathed and hated by your own; to you, I say: you are a lucky one. You can be one more among us. Not better or worse, not bigger or smaller, not wealthier or poorer, just one more among us. One of the chosen. Look here: you have now found your shelter, the shield you were looking for even before you were born.

Enrique - It's a mermaid's song.

Yolanda - No. It's a constant opportunity. A daily chance. Here, it can happen. Everything can happen here.

Enrique - (To the audience.) My castle is not so big. Three rooms. Not so comfortable, either. . . (A train goes by.) It's built next to a train line. Sometimes, it sounds as if it were built under the train line. When one sleeps, one dreams with earthquakes, seaquakes and worldquakes. Yolanda. . . (A train goes by.) Yolanda. . . Do you like these trains?

Yolanda - (Conciliatory) They are not a great nuisance.

Enrique - (Smiles.) Women. Ah, women. My castle has three padlocks. (Two steps.) It has a balcony, where one can chat from time to time. . . (An airplane goes by.) When there are no planes over the roof. In good weather, we hear a plane every minute. In the summer, in the hellish heath of summer. When a. . . (Train.) A train goes by, you cannot chat. And when a plane goes by. . . (Plane.) You can never talk, as I was saying, with so many planes up there and so many trains down here.

Yolanda - Al mal tiempo, buena cara.

Cecilia - Good morning, Dad. Good morning. Good morning, New York!

Enrique - When you talk about New York, you are not talking about New York, really. There's no such thing as New York. It's only a Utopian dream, an impossible dream. When you talk about New York, you are talking about

Manhattan. Manhattan is a monument, like another monument, Disneyworld. Who wants to live in Disneyworld?

Cecilia - I wanna live in Disneyworld!

Alejo - I want to live in Disneyworld!

Little Vera - . . .wanna live in Disneyworld!

Cecilia - The whole world wants to live in Disneyworld!

Enrique - But. . . One cannot live in Disneyworld. One can visit Disneyworld, spend a few days in Disneyworld, perhaps. . . It may be possible. But nobody can live in Disneyworld.

Vera - Why?

Enrique - Because it's not for real. . . Its a dream. . . A dream made of plastic and steel.

Children - Let's go to Disneyworld! Let's go to Manhattan!

Vera - Let's live all of our dreams and hopes!

Voices - Let's live a million year holiday!

Enrique - Who is paying for it?

Yolanda - Children, school time is here. Are you ready?

Children - We are! Bye, Dad. Bye, Mom.

Cecilia - See you tonight!

Yolanda - Sleep well, Enrique.

(They leave. Enrique stands alone, his arms hanging, he is tired. Three steps toward the table. He sits on the chair. Sighs. A plane goes by. He lights a cigarette. Smokes. Looks around. Smokes. A very noisy train. He does not move for a few seconds. Trains and planes make such noise that human voices could not be heard. He smokes. Unwillingly, he turns to the table. He puts a "paper" in the typewriter. Puts the cigarette down. Begins to type. He works for a while. When he is lost in his work, a train goes by. He smokes. He reads. He denies with his head. He rips the paper from the typewriter. Smokes. He sets another paper. A plane. He waits until the plane goes by. He smokes. He looks at the paper. He scratches the outside of his hand. He stands. He plays with his clothes. He scratches his head. He opens his shirt. He loosens his belt. A train. A plane. He sits. Hesitantly, he types. He reads. He rips the paper from the machine. Smokes. Blows the smoke to the ceiling.

He sets another paper. A plane. He looks at the ceiling, waiting. The noise fades off. He starts again, but a train goes by. He stands. He walks around. He fades among the shadows. Slam of a door.

Enrique enters under a light. He sits. He stretches his arms, plays with his fingers, like a piano player. He tries to start. A train. He hits the table with his fingers. A cigarette. He lights it. Looks at the paper. He lays his chin on his hands. With one finger, he tries a few letters, slowly. He straightens himself. He attempts to start again.

He starts. He writes a paragraph. A plane. He goes on. A train. He goes on. A plane. He goes on. The phone. He goes on. A plane. He stops. He crosses his arms. He reads. He scratches his nose. The phone stops rinsing. He smokes. He writes again. A plane. He stops. He puts his hands against his ears. He tears his hair. A long train. He stands in anguish. He throws his fists against the sky. He walks fast, fades off again. A door is slammed. A plane. A slow train. A fire truck. A police siren. A car honks in rhythm. A plane. A TV announcer fades on and gets higher and higher. Other radio and TV voices and noises. All noise make one strong noise which raises until it harms our ears and then subsides almost to silence.

Light. From center back, Enrique enters dressed with a poncho and an Indian cap, a black blanket in his arm. He is chewing. He walks and lays the blanket with an ample gesture and he sits behind it, Oriental fashion. He has an Indian bag. A "Ileechlla." He opens a big white kerchief on the blanket. He takes a handful of small green leaves from the Ileehlla. Mumbles a few noises and throws the leaves in front of him, watching carefully while they fall on the kerchief. He mumbles other noises. He is still chewing. A sad music. Pentatonic. He does not move, but we see his chewing. He studies carefully each and every leaf. He "reads" the leaves. He mumbles a few noises. With ample gestures, he lights a cigarette and smokes it slowly by the middle of his mouth, holding it with his midfinger and his thumb, other fingers open. He throws big smoke clouds to the ceiling and reads the smoke. He works at his chewing. He grabs another handful of leaves and throws it to the air, so that they fall on the kerchief. He reads them. He watches them. He chews. He smokes. He closes his eyes. He says a few Spanish words out of context. He opens his eyes and talks to the audience.)

Enrique - I am following an old piece of advice. . . An old consolation

offered by my grandfather, Don Humberto Enrique, whom God may keep in His Glory. "When things get too difficult, my son," he used to say, "turn to mother earth. Pachamama. Turn your eyes to the earth. Turn your soul to the earth. Fix your spirit on the earth. On the earth you were born on."
(For a few minutes, he follows this ritual. With care, he picks up his leaves and saves some in his Ileechlla).

Enrique - I would have been this man if the Spaniards had never arrived. I would have been like this if Columbus' ships had sunk, if God had pity on a whole continent and the black fever had taken Don Cristobal to Hell. . . Or the Great Ocean Sea had been far bigger. . . Like this, like you see me, I would have been, had God decided not to put an end to the Age of Innocence. . . Had He decided not to ever create white men. . . Had He decided not to allow an eternal genocide for red men, for copper-men and black men. . .

This is me, innocent me, had Francisco Pizarro died with a kind hepatitis, had Vasco de Gama died in his cradle, had Gonzalo Pizarro broken his neck, had Pedrarias never set foot on Panama. . . If Cortez had not burnt his ships, if the Moors had not lost Granada, if Magellan had looked the other way, if Atahuallpa had ordered thirteen murderers murdered. . . And everybody would be singing those monotonous legends about the old and extinct white tribes that used to live in the northern snows. . .

This is me if the world was not the toy of the great white barbarian, the latter-day barbarian, the kingdom of the great white god. . . If the great soulless legions had been wiped out by some benevolent white disease. . . If gods old and new could not be mad too. (Smokes.)

Enrique - (When he talks, he shows what he is talking about.) This is a Iloojchoo. It's wonderful for the snow of the Andes. This is a poncho, as you know. Everybody likes a good poncho. And this is coca. It is very well known up there that, the day coca leaves leave our mountains to go everywhere and to conquer everybody, such will be the day of the end of the world. Well, known by everybody among us. I chew coca leaves to feel powerful , people say. Not just powerful, but at peace. Also, but only from time to time, to disguise hunger.

But I don't just chew these leaves. I akoolleeko. Yes, I a-koo-llee-ko. Kallawayas in my land have been doing akulleekos for centuries now. Green akoolleekos like this. . . (He half opens his mouth and shows a green ball made of leaves.)

Ka-lla-wa-yas, yes. That's it: that is how you pronounce it. Kallawayas are magi. Great physicians. Wise doctors. A tribe of magi and physicians. Friends of the earth with the earth as their friend and master. They are still walking up there, following old paths in the Andean mountains, with their magical tools and their akoolleekos here. (Shows the bag.) This is my lleehlla. Kallawayas perform real miracles, as does every true magus. (Smokes.) Coca is magical too. I throw the coca leaves like this.. They fall like this, and I can read my days to come in these leaves. . . My future and everybody's days to come. . . (Smokes.) I mean, I could read all that if I was a Ka-lla-wa-ya, which I am not. And if I knew how to akulleeking as the Pachamama commands, which I don't know. And if I was my grandfather's grandfather, which I am not. . .

But nothing can stop me from sitting like this, as my great-grandfather used to sit, or from chewing coca like this, like the first Kallawaya did, or from reading like this. . . (he throws the leaves to the air and the handkerchief.) My coca leaves. Nothing can stop me from saying once again, as if I knew what I was doing:

(Inhales. Closes his eyes. Pause).

Ama Sua - Ama Lloolla - Ama Kaella. (Pause. Opens his eyes. Slight smile.)

I learned those words at school. When I was eight. It's the first law of the man of copper. Ama Sua - don't be lazy. Ama Lloolla - don't steal. Ama Kaella - don't tell lies.

Easy, right? Three commandments only. . . Not ten, or fifteen, as those from the most modern gods. (Smokes, looks around.) Now, everything is quite. . . (Police car far away.) It's three o'clock. Everybody sleeps. Or naps. They may be far away, working. So it seems. Trains come by five. Planes come by sundown as does television with the children, when they come back from school. But until then. . . (Smokes.) I can akulleeking, I read my fate in the coca leaves, I smoke and I pray the First Law. It soothes my nerves.

(He starts again with this ritual. Chews. Smokes. Throws the leaves over the kerchief. Mumbles words and noises. The music goes on. Pause. A train approaches from the right, goes through with a great noise, fades to the left. Enrique closes and opens his eyes. He tries to ignore the noises. He launches a handful of leaves. He chews. He smokes. A train. Another train. A long train. Enrique attempts to ignore everything but his ritual, listening only to the music. He looks to the audience in search of understanding.)

Enrique - Reading coca is not difficult. One needs only to watch the ways in which they lay. Face to you, side to you, front, backside, north-northeast, south-southeast, to my chest.

Everything has a meaning, nothing comes by chance. Everything is in these leaves. Everything talks through these coca leaves, everything can be read here. . . A clear message for every living being. (A train.) Inside my head, because I akoolleeko, there's silence, order, harmony, like when I was a child. (A train.)

There is great consolation in the ways by which these leaves drop to the earth. . . They are like the words of God, like a letter from distant relatives we used to love, from those who wait for us in the other shore. . . These leaves talk to us. . . (A train.) It must be five o'clock by now, damn it. . . Not only do they talk about the past and about the present, but about the future. . . about what fate was given to our dead. . . But I cannot read these leaves. . . I cannot read what they are saying to me about the dead, our dead. . .
.

I would like to see, if I akulleeko, if I akulleeko with all my heart, if I akulleeko with sheer desperation. . . I may be able to see, I say, if I akulleeko to keep but these leaves, the smoke of this cigar and the lights that blow inside my head. . . (A train.) I can see whatever has been, what is and what will be. . . By chewing. . . (A train. Enrique waits for the noise to fade out.) And by listening to the wind, eternal wind of our music, my music. . . (A train.) Akoolleeking, smoking, looking at these leaves, at the smoke. . . (He remains static. Trains, planes, trucks, cars and other noises keep coming and going until their noise dominates the place.)

Enrique - (Opens his eyes. Looks far away, in the void.) The voices of my dead people. The voices I tried to keep in my memory in spite of everything. . . The voices that should have followed me forever and everywhere, that should have talked, lived in me. . . So that I could copy their echoes whenever I could find an instant of peace and silence. . . The voices of my dead. . . Voices that go now, that are going far away now, as rags of my old skin, with every train and every noise that harms my ears. . . My mind. . . (A train.)

Now I cannot hear the moaning of my children anymore, that horrible hour in which the soldiers went into the mine and the miners waited for their murderers with nothing but three dynamite sticks and their women and their children as witnesses, their children, my children, waiting for their killers and their planes, and howitzers, machine guns, tanks. . . For their killers, drugged and always thirsty. . . I cannot hear their howling anymore, their voices are not here anymore, their screams, their passion and their deaths, their heroism and their courage. . . (Far, almost muted. An explosion, screams, machine gun fire.) Their voices, their names, their death. Their death. . . (A train, with a great noise.) I cannot hear anything now.

I cannot see, now, the clear faces of the people who shared with me the gray sun of exile, the cigarettes, so many cells, those cells made of frozen raindrops and wooden doors, big colonial padlocks, those men with dirty overcoats, a rifle over their shoulders and a bestial laugh in the middle of the night. . . I cannot see as clear as usual the laughing face of my executioners, those I saw when they were killing. . . Those who. . . That man, let's say. . . The man who killed Mamani when I was. . . Who killed Mamani? How could I forget him? How could I forget him? How could I forget him, my God? (Hides his face in his hands. A train goes by.)

Their struggles had to be told, I had to shout their battles' echoes, just those echoes, echoes of their heroic deeds. . . I had to relive the suffering in the cells, I had to see once again the shooting, the killings, they made them eat powder, they made them eat powder. . . I had to. . . I had to. . . (A train.) I had to. . . I had to. . . What? It's after five. After five already.

I remember that man who saw his dying brother.. Who tried to kill a tyrant because he saw his brother's death. . . It was a very sad story, a story so sad. . . A very good story such good story. . . It's a shame. It's is shame, this forgetting just like this, just because a train goes by, and another train goes by and still another, another train always.. (A train.) To forget who that man was, and why he tried to kill the tyrant, and what is the end of everything. . . (A train.) There's no place here for us human beings. (A train.) But there's no place to hide, anymore. No place to hide. Help. (A train.) Its six o'clock. Help. Its seven o'clock. Help. Ya son las siete. Socorro. And you'll eat your everynight bread with the sweating of your forehead. Help.

Yolanda - Hey, children. How are you? How was everything today?

Alejo - We read about the galaxies today.

Cecilia - We spoke about the hydrogen bomb today.

Vera - We went to the space museum today.

Yolanda - All right. And now we all go shopping to Macy's.

Enrique - Help.

Yolanda - Enrique, so many cockroaches. What's wrong with the car?

Enrique - We are all cockroaches. Help.

Vera - When are we going to Disneyworld?

Alejo - I need an Atari!

Cecilia - I need a computer!

Enrique - Help. No akulleeko can work here.

Yolanda - I need a Cuisinart!

Vera - Let's go to Miami!

Alejo - How about a Betamax!

Vera - I need a bike!

Alejo - Me too!

Enrique - Help. (A plane.) The planes are here. Help.

Yolanda - Enrique, what are you doing? Don't lose your time. Nobody loses time here. You must work tonight. You must leave at eight. Be ready, now.

Enrique - The planes. Help.

Cecilia - What's that funny cap? Take that thing off your head, Dad.

Enrique - Funny cap? Funny cap. . . This is no funny cap, you ignorant brat, this is a Iloohchoo!

Cecilia - A what?

Enrique - (He takes it off) Bah. You'll never understand. . . (He wears it again.)

Cecilia - Nobody can understand that thing. A. . . What?

Enrique - Its quite comfortable. And very useful in cold weather. It was your grandfather's Iloojchoo.

Vera - My grandfather. . . (Screams.) Hey, Mom! He's saying I had a grandpa!

Yolanda - Everybody has a grandpa, dear.

Vera - Dana has no grandparents. Cheng has no grandparents. Ramiro has no grandparents. I have no grandparents. Nobody has grandparents.

Alejo - Linda has no grandparents. She never had grandparents!

Yolanda - We all have grandparents, but some children never met theirs.

Vera - Look at Dad! How funny you look, Dad, with that tat on your head!

Enrique - I was thinking. . .

Vera - Take that cap off your head!

Alejo - And that dirty rag too. Such an old, ugly rag! Take it off.

Enrique - It's not ugly.

Yolanda - It would look better on the wall, hanging there.

Alejo - Like a hunting trophy.

Enrique - Hanging there? Are you crazy? How can you think about hanging my grandfather's poncho on the wall?

Cecilia - It would be better to hang it there, I say. It would be like a bizarre ornament.

Enrique - I won't allow you to. . . (A train.) Help.

Yolanda - And those leaves, What are those leaves?

Enrique - (Hesitantly.) I was akoolleeking.

Alejo - Aku. . .. What?

Yolanda - You are mad, Enrique! What are you doing with those things here? Those things. . . In front of the children. . . Throw those leaves away!

Enrique - But. . . But, Yolanda. . .

Yolanda - Enough of your madness. Throw those leaves to the trash. Right away!

Enrique - But. . . But. . . But! (A plane.) Help.

Yolanda - Nobody does such things anymore. Nobody believes those superstitions. Enrique, you must go to work tonight.

Enrique - Please. . . Yolanda. . .

Alejo - Throw those leaves to the trash, Mom says!

Vera - Flashtime! (Combat sounds in the TV.) Flash, the Avenger!

Yolanda - What are we having for dinner?

Enrique - Dinner? Dinner? I have had no dinner since we arrived! I spend my whole life eating hot dogs and cold drinks. . . (A plane.) Help.

Yolanda - Don't complain. Everybody eats junk food at work. That's enough.

Enrique - But I want a steak!

Yolanda - Steak? Who has time for a steak? I work and take care of this place. There's no time for any steak..

Cecilia - Eat a snack!

Alejo - Get a Coke!

Vera - Have a cheese sandwich!

Yolanda - Look in the freezer. There must be something there. Why are you so useless? If I don't cook for you. . . (A train.)

Enrique - Help.

Yolanda - Stand up, Enrique. Its about time.

Enrique - But. . . But.

Yolanda - No buts here. Here, things are quite different. Life is hard and work is tough. But we have everything here. Everything is here, whatever you may want.

Cecilia - Everything. . . and more!

Yolanda - Hard work and discipline. That's the key. Come, children.

Enrique - (Stands up. Takes his Iloohchoo off. Takes his poncho off. He makes a bundle and throws it away.) Who will be here tomorrow, when I come back?

Yolanda - We cannot be here; we work and study.

Vera - Viva! I'll go to Manhattan!

Alejo - I'll see the Brooklyn Bridge!

Cecilia - Viva Manhattan!

Enrique - Nobody here when I come back? Nobody, once more? (A plane.) Help.

(A TV commercial. "This is it." The children sing with the TV.)

Children - This is it. This is it. This is it!

Enrique - But. . . But wait, children. . . I can never talk to you. . .

Children - No time; we work and study.

Cecilia - Besides, you work every night, always. . . Every night.

Enrique - You mean you have no time at all for your own father?

Yolanda - No. We work hard and we play hard.

Enrique - Yolanda? You too? (A train.)

Yolanda and Children - Yes. All of us.

Enrique - What are you learning?

Yolanda and Children - I am, you are, he is, she is, it is, we are, we are, we are, we are, WE ARE, WE ARE, WE ARE, (other voices sing this sound together.)

Choir - WE ARE, WE ARE, WE ARE, WE ARE!

(A train. The TV makes noises, voices and lights. The choir keeps yelling. A plane. A Police car. A fire truck. A plane. A train. While these noises come and go, Enrique starts wearing his new uniform, that of a working man. A steel cap, blue jeans, a handkerchief hanging from his back pocket, boots. A strong coat. He puts a chewing gum in his mouth and chews it. When the sounds end abruptly, Enrique turns around and looks at the audience, expressionless. He holds one hand against his head, two fingers on his right eyebrow.)

Enrique - Yep.

(Darkness).

Ten Years Later....

South

Character	Scene	Nationality	Born in
Admiral	The Skin	Bolivia	La Paz
Alejo	The Coup	USA	Bolivia
Ambassador (Perú)	Exile	Perú	Lima
Anita	Victims	Bolivia	La Paz
Atlas	Capture	Bolivia	La Paz
Augustine	The Skin	Spain	Spain
Baker	The Skin	Bolivia	La Paz
Baker Woman	Massacre	Bolivia	La Paz
Benavidez	Capture	Bolivia	La Paz
Butcher	Massacre	Bolivia	Cbba.
Campesino	Massacre	Bolivia	Oruro
Capataz (municipal)	The Skin	Bolivia	La Paz
Carabinero	Massacre	Bolivia	La Paz
Carabinero (Police)	Massacre	Bolivia	La Paz
Caracoles Women	Massacre	Bolivia	
Cecilia	The Coup	USA	Bolivia
Chola	The Skin	Bolivia	Andes
Clerk	Massacre	Bolivia	La Paz
Cochabamba			
Daniel	Capture	Bolivia	La Paz
Diego de Almagro	The Skin	Spain	Spain
Diplomat	The Skin	Bolivia	Sta. Cruz
Doctor (Family)	Exile	Bolivia	La Paz
Doctor (Ginecology)	The Skin	Bolivia	Sta. Cruz
Dominican	The Skin	Spain	Spain
Doorman	Capture	Bolivia	La Paz
Driver	Massacre	Bolivia	La Paz
Drug Baron	The Skin	Bolivia	Sta. Cruz
Editor	Exile	Bolivia	La Paz
Enrique	The Coup	Bolivia	La Paz
Enrique Peñaranda	The Skin	Bolivia	Tarata
Entrepeneur (Import)	The Skin	Bolivia	La Paz

Age   Ten Years later

Age	Ten Years later
?	Drowned. Titicaca Lake.
9	London School of Economics.
-	Deceased. Lima.
-	Desaparecida.
46	Famous Torturer. Vanished.
-	
64	Baker. La Paz.
-	Deceased. La Paz.
58	Famous Torturer. Vanished.
43	Butcher. Cochabamba.
-	Deceased. Oruro.
49	Handicapted. Right Leg.
40	Carabinero. La Paz.
43	Carabinero. La Paz.
-	Caracoles. Bolivia.
10	Law Student. Los Angeles.
?	Cook. La Paz.
-	Deceased. La Paz.
	City in Bolivia. The Valley.
36	Salesman. La Paz.
-	Pizarro's Partner. 80
39	Teacher. Santa Cruz.
57	Doctor. La Paz.
45	Ambassador. Hungary.
-	
57	Doorman. La Paz.
-	Deceased. Oruro.
66	Presidential Candidate (Thrice)
55	Ambassador. Washington.
44	Blind. Cochabamba.
-	President. Gave tin away.1935 (?)
48	Hotel Owner. Santa Cruz

South

Character	Scene	Nationality	
Fernando	Victims	Bolivia	La Paz
Franciscano	The Skin	Spain	Spain
Francisco Pizarro	The Skin	Spain	Spain
General (Air Force)	The Skin	Bolivia	La Paz
Gentleman (Mining)	The Skin	Bolivia	Oruro
Germán Busch	The Skin	Bolivia	Bolivia
Green Berret	The Skin		
Indian	The Skin	Bolivia	La Paz
Indian Child	The Skin		
Indian Shepperd	The Skin	Bolivia	La Paz
Inquisitor	The Skin		
Journalist	The Skin		
Juan Carlos	Victims	Bolivia	La Paz
Judge	The Skin	Bolivia	Cbba.
Julio	Victims	Bolivia	La Paz
Kiko	The Skin	Bolivia	Oruro
Kollasuyo			
Kuraka	The Skin	Bolivia	Oruro
La Paz			
Lady	The Skin	Bolivia	La Paz
Lawyer (Civil)	The Skin	Bolivia	La Paz
Loayza (Coronel)	Capture	Bolivia	La Paz
Luis Recio de León	The Skin	Spain	Spain
Mamani	Hounds	Bolivia	La Paz
Martín de Robles	The Skin		
Mayor	The Skin	Bolivia	Uyuni
Medic (Military)	Hounds	Bolivia	La Paz
Melchor de Rodas	The Skin		
Mercenario	The Skin	Argentina	?
Military (Army)	The Skin		
Miner Woman	Massacre	Bolivia	Oruro
Miss Spring	The Skin	Bolivia	Sta. Cruz

Age   Ten Years later

Age	Ten Years later
-	Desaparecido.
-	
-	Conquered Inca Empire with 13 men.
-	Land Owner. Santa Cruz.
54	Retired. Canary Islands.
-	President. Nationalized Oil. Murdered.
	Político Security. La Paz.
-	Aymara Group - Larecaja.
	Symbol, out of fashion
25	Symbol, out of fashion
	No witch burning in Kollasuyo.
47	Inmigrant. USA
-	Deceased. La Paz.
56	Retired. Santa Cruz.
-	Deceased. La Paz.
39	Miami, USA (?)
	Inca Name for Bolivia
50	Kuraka. Indian Chieftain.
	City in Bolivia. The Mountain.
48	Housekeeper. La Paz.
50	Exile. Chile.
60	Famous Torturer. Vanished.
-	142
-	Desaparecido.
	90
63	Trader (Beer). Uyuni.
?	MIA (?)
	101
?	?
	Retired. Oruro.
57	Road Worker. Copenhague
26	Rural Teacher. Cochabamba.

South

Character	Scene	Nationality	
Nuflo de Chavez	The Skin	Spain	Spain
Old Man	Massacre	Bolivia	La Paz
Old Man (Gardener)	The Skin	Bolivia	La Paz
Old Woman	Massacre	Bolivia	La Paz
Old Woman	Massacre	Bolivia	Oruro
Oruro			
Pedro de Anzúrez	The Skin	Spain	Spain
Policeman (Urban)	The Skin	Bolivia	La Paz
Priest	The Skin	Bolivia	Spain
Priest	Massacre	Spain	Spain
Private (Army)	Massacre	Bolivia	La Paz
Private (Army)	Exile	Bolivia	Oruro
Rancher (Meat)	The Skin	Bolivia	Beni
Ranger	The Coup	Bolivia	La Paz
Ranger (corporal)	Massacre	Bolivia	La Paz
Red Berret	Masacre	Bolivia	La Paz
Red Berret	Masacre	Bolivia	La Paz
Red Berret	Capture	Bolivia	Beni
Reporter (Woman)	Exile	Bolivia	Cbba.
Roberto	Victims	Bolivia	La Paz
Rubber Worker	The Skin	Bolivia	Beni
Sailor	Hounds	Bolivia	Cbba.
Sailor	Massacre	Bolivia	La Paz
Salesman (Shoes)	The Skin	Bolivia	Sucre
Santa Cruz			
Scholar (History)	The Skin	Bolivia	La Paz
Scholar (Physics)	The Skin	Bolivia	La Paz
Schoolboy	Massacre	Bolivia	La Paz
Schoolboy	The Skin	Bolivia	La Paz
Secretary (Health)	The Skin	Bolivia	Cbba.
Simón I. Patiño	The Skin		
Student (Law)	The Skin	Bolivia	Oruro

Age   **Ten Years later**

Age	Ten Years later
-	Fundó Santa Cruz.
-	Deceased. La Paz.
65	Deceased. TB.
-	Deceased. Oruro.
69	Beggar. La Paz.
	City in Bolivia. Mines.
-	Explored Beni (Oriental Jungle)
37	Urban Police. La Paz.
39	Parson. Madrid.
-	Desaparecido.
33	Captain. La Paz.
33	Indian Community, Poopo Lake
61	Local Drug Baron. (Cocaine). Beni.
22	Customs Clerk. La Paz.
45	Military Attache. (?)
38	General Store. Oruro.
44	Lawyer. La Paz.
-	?
45	Cultural Attache. Washington.
-	Desaparecido.
?	?
48	Vice-Admiral. La Paz.
-	?
34	Sales. Kitchenware. La Paz.
	City in Bolivia. The Plains.
40	Cuba (?)
56	Consul, Asunción.
22	University Student. La Paz
25	Mining Engineering Student. Hungary.
40	Social Worker. Cochabamba.
-	Legendary Tin King
19	Representative. No degree.

South

Character	Scene	Nationality	
Student (Law) Sucre	Massacre	Bolivia	La Paz
Taylor	Massacre	Bolivia	La Paz
Teacher	The Skin	Bolivia	La Paz
Teacher (Math)	The Skin	Bolivia	La Paz
Teacher (Sewing)	The Skin	Bolivia	Sucre
Teacher (Woman)	The Skin	Bolivia	Oruro
Teacher (Woman)	Massacre	Bolivia	La Paz
Tourist	The Skin	USA	Boston
Truck Driver	The Skin	Bolivia	Cbba.
Tupac Katari	The Skin	Kollasuyo	Andes
Vasquez de Urrea	The Skin		
Vera	The Coup	USA	La Paz
Virrey Toledo	The Skin		
Woman	Victims	Bolivia	Yungas
Worker	Massacre	Bolivia	Oruro
Worker (Iron)	The Skin	Bolivia	Oruro
Worker (Oil)	The Skin	Bolivia	Sta.Ana
Yolanda	The Coup	USA	La Paz

Age   Ten Years later

Age	Ten Years later
32	Driver. La Paz.
	Capital City, Bolivia
44	Retired. (blind.)
54	Teacher. La Paz.
44	Professor (Math.) La Paz.
-	Deceased. La Paz.
32	Teacher. Oruro.
53	Maid. Paris.
51	Tourist. Asunción (?)
45	Businessman (Beer) La Paz.
-	Indian Rebel, 1544
	114
8	Artist. New York City.
-	Deceased. La Paz.
-	Deceased. La Paz.
35	Deceased. Accident. La Paz.
46	Trader (Leather)
37	Teacher. Cochabamba.

North

Character	Scene	Nationality	Born in
Abel	Office	USA	Argentina
Adalberto Pando	Neighb'ood	USA	Cuzco
Alberto	Office	USA	P. Rico
Alex Ruiz	Subway	USA	Panamá
Atleta	Train	USA	Perth
Beggar Woman	Train	USA	KansasCity
Blas Ramirez	Neighb'ood	USA	Panamá
Blind (false)	Train	Chile	Santiago
Body Builder	Train	USA	Brooklyn
Boy with Guitar	Train	USA	Provo
Carlos	Office	USA	Argentina
Carlos Teruel	Neighb'ood	Spain	Madrid
Casildo Herrera	Subway	USA	Chile
Construction Worker	Train	USA	New Mexico
Cowboy	Train	USA	Miami
Dandy	Train	USA	Havana
Darío Perez	Subway	USA	Caracas
Darío Roncal	Subway	USA	San Juan
Dr. Bernal	Neighb'ood	USA	Potosí
Dr. Ferrufino	Neighb'ood	Bolivia	Oruro
Dr. Martínez	Subway	USA	Chile
Driver	G.Central	USA	Montevideo
El Michi	Subway	?	?
Eloy Blasco	Neighb'ood	USA	Baires
Eva Gonzalez	Subway	USA	Baires
Federico Troche	Subway	Perú	Cuzco
Felipe Alcón	Subway	USA	Nicaragua
Felipe Ostos	Neighb'ood	España	Toledo
Felix	Office	Perú	Lima
Felix Coronado	Subway	Bolivia	Sta. Cruz
Germán	Office	Perú	Lima
Girl	Subway	-	-

Age	Ten Years Later
49	Journalist. Miami.
36	Sales. Cars. Queens.
26	Barman. Manhattan.
-	Deceased. AIDS.
28	Lifesaver. Los Angeles.
59	Beggar. Washington.
34	Cook. Harlem.
36	Blind. New Jersey.
35	Extra. Hollywood.
23	Singer. Los Angeles.
43	Translator. Washington.
45	Waiter. Manhattan.
36	Almacenero. Queens.
38	Indian Reservation.
37	Rodeo. Texarkana.
32	Murdered. Manhattan.
34	Representative. Caracas
29	Singer. Miami.
41	Lawyer. NYC.
46	Lorton Jail. Drug Charges.
-	?
39	Driver. Brooklyn
?	?
39	Radio Announcer. Seattle.
33	Dancer. Miami.
32	Cook. Arlington VA
37	Teacher. Managua.
35	Waiter. Las Vegas.
45	Reporter. México City.
42	Deceased. Queens.
43	Travel Agent. Chicago.
5	Symbol, our of fashion

North

Character	Scene	Nationality	Born in
Gordo	Train	USA	Queens
Gustavo	Office	USA	Bolivia
Gustavo Sotelo	G.Central	Perú	Arequipa
Hermes Cortéz	Neighb'ood	Perú	Arequipa
Hernán Pereira	Neighb'ood	Salvador	Salvador
Jack Mamani	Neighb'ood	USA	Oruro
Jaime Perez	Neighb'ood	México	?
Jesus Ruiz	Neighb'ood	USA	Paita
Johnny Paz	G.Central	Bolivia	Sucre
Jorge	Office	USA	Paraguay
Jorge Luiz	Neighb'ood	USA	Río
José Bonilla	G.Central	Costa Rica	San José
José del Granado	Subway	USA	Bolivia
Juan "Seis Dedos"	Subway	Cuba	Cuba
Juan Calderón	Neighb'ood	USA	La Paz
Juan Franco	Subway	México	Tijuana
Juan Rodriguez	G.Central	Salvador	?
Juan Ruiz	Neighb'ood	USA	Valparaíso
Lawyer	G.Central	USA	Chile
Lucero Peralta	Subway	USA	México
Lucho Campos	Neighb'ood	USA	Quito
Lucho Vidal	Neighb'ood	USA	Lima
Lucinda Real	Subway	Cuba	Havana
Luis	Oficina	USA	Chile
Luis Bocangel	Neighb'ood	Dominicana	?
Luis Paniagua	Subway	Paraguay	Asunción
Luis Tirado	Neighb'ood	Paraguay	Asunción
Luisa Tovar	Subway	USA	Argentina
Man in Black	Train	USA	Manila
Man with Beard	Train	USA	Moscú
Man with Books	Train	USA	Arequipa
Man with Flowers	Train	USA	Cabo Frío

Age   Ten Years Later

Age	Ten Years Later
34	Saxo Player. Hollywood.
44	Reporter. Cochabamba.
45	Murdered. Queens.
37	Doctor. Brooklyn.
34	Jobless. Salvador.
32	Palm Beach. (Lottery).
43	Mariachi. NYC.
41	Car Mechanic. Queens.
36	Artist. Soho.
38	Mayor. Asunción.
34	Deceased. Accident.
56	Jeweler. Manhattan.
48	Cook. Manhattan.
36	Murdered. Washington.
34	Doorman. Manhattan.
42	?
36	Jobless. Bronx.
33	Mariachi. Manhattan.
52	Lawyer. NYC.
34	Sales. Queens.
43	Artist. Los Angeles.
45	Photography. Queens.
33	Housekeeper. Havana.
45	Reporter. Miami.
34	?
43	Sailor. Marseille.
39	Doctor. Asunción.
36	Sales. Cars. Los Angeles.
45	Actor. Los Angeles.
33	Language Teacher. Manhattan.
36	Programmer. Manhattan.
29	?

North

Character	Scene	Nationality	Born in
Man with Violin Box	Train	USA	San Diego
Marina Delgado	Neighb'ood	Ecuador	Quito
Mario	Office	Cuba	?
Mario Arauco	G.Central	USA	Montevideo
María Lopez	G.Central	Dominicana	?
Midget with Cigar	Train	France	Paris
Nun with Painted Lips	Train	USA	Toronto
Old Homosexual	Train	USA	Lima
Old Woman	G.Central	Argentina	?
Orfeo Angeluz	Neighb'ood	USA	San José
Pablo Curcio	G.Central	España	?
Patricia	Office	USA	Ecuador
Pedro Ocampo	Neighb'ood	Nicaragua	Managua
Pedro Triana	Neighb'ood	USA	Bogotá
Preacher with Bible	Train	USA	La Paz
Priest with Eyepatch	Train	USA	Las Vegas
Prof. Anaya	Neighb'ood	Bolivia	Sucre
Ramiro Lopera	Subway	USA	Oruro
Rex Rodo	Neighb'ood	USA	Tarma
Ricardo Gomez	Subway	USA	Bogotá
Ricardo Gomez	Subway	Argentina	Rioja
Ricardo Tapia	Neighb'ood	Bolivia	Oruro
Rigoberto Diaz	Subway	Colombia	Bogotá
Rita Ruibal	Neighb'ood	USA	San Juan
Roberto Sacoto	G.Central	USA	?
Robertson Gamboa	Subway	USA	Quito
Ronald Villarroel	Subway	USA	Paita
Roque Arias	Subway	Salvador	Salvador
Safari Guide	Train	USA	Chicago
Salesman	G.Central	USA	Cuba
Sandro Careaga	Neighb'ood	Colombia	Medellín
Santiago Najar	Subway	USA	Guatemala

Age   Ten Years Later

Age	Ten Years Later
36	Deceased. AIDS.
34	Nurse. Queens.
29	Businessman. Miami.
32	Deceased. AIDS.
36	Murdered. Bronx.
?	Circo Americano. London.
26	Missionary. Brasil.
69	Motel Manager. NYC.
-	Vanished. Mahattan.
34	Artist. San José.
43	Desaparecido.
34	Journalist. Washington.
51	Printer. Queens.
43	Jeweler. Manhattan.
32	Protestant Priest. Miami.
35	Mental Hospital. NYC.
34	English Teacher. Sucre.
29	Driver. Washington.
23	Waiter. Manhattan.
36	Dentist. Bronx.
34	Gaucho Singer. Manhattan.
29	Nurse. Bronx.
-	Murdered. Bogotá.
43	Teacher. Bronx.
?	?
32	Murdered. Washington.
38	"Strip Girl". Bronx.
27	Jobless. NYC.
?	?
38	Deceased. AIDS.
37	Jeweler. Queens.
34	Waiter. Bronx.

North

Character	Scene	Nationality	Born in
Secretaria	G.Central	USA	Colombia
Sra. Ferrufino	Neighb'ood	USA	Mendoza
Ursula Romero	G.Central	USA	Panama
Widow	Train	USA	Dallas
Woman in Furs	Train	USA	Miami
Woman in Sleeping...	Train	USA	Cairo
Woman with Radio Box	Train	USA	St.Louis
Young Homosexual	Train	Perú	Lima

Age	Ten Years Later
36	Secretary. Brooklyn.
37	Housekeeper. Queens.
32	Dancer. Manhattan
-	Deceased. Dallas.
32	Beggar. Manhattan.
36	Mental Hospital. NYC.
32	Deceased. AIDS.
19	Deceased. AIDS.

A Story You will
Never see in the Papers

..

On My Broken English

The Million Dollar Wall

This first vice began half a century ago and when I was five, thanks to Donald Duck.

I remember that afternoon as if it were yesterday. We went to the tiny second-hand bookstore in the shadow of the Miraflores soccer stadium and my father read a big poster that said: "Donald Duck comes to Bolivia! He comes next week, so boys and girls, be ready to welcome Donald!" He was coming via some weekly comic books printed in Argentina.

It was great news indeed, but I was not ready: I could not read. So, while we walked back home, we made a deal. My father would teach me to read in seven days, no matter what it took. It took him smacking me with his knuckles on my head each time I made a mistake, but I learned to read in a week. So, when Donald came to Bolivia I bought that first issue and followed him and his nephews for the next 14 years. I have never stopped reading since then. You could say that I read all the time, no matter where I am.

My second vice began about two years later, when I wrote my first "poem". It took 32 pages of a big notebook. It was written for a very sweet girl who couldn't care less for my humble person, so perhaps she was no more than an excuse. Thank God I lost that notebook a few weeks later, but I remember it well, quite well. Back then writing was sheer joy and nothing was as wonderful as reading what came from nowhere as a dust of dreams on a white page to turn itself into very black things that you could never change once they stared back at you from the page, free and immortal a second after you had made them. I remember all of them, these words made by my fingers over forty years as a journalist and in two dozen books, published and/or saved in my computer diskettes. I write a page or two every day. Most of it never reaches a piece of paper. It goes directly to my digital trash file. These days, I am the writer and the first and last reader of my digital words. It is still a vice and I enjoy it as if I were five years old. I laugh and get sad, and smile and cry and sometimes my laughter makes my wife come and ask, "What? What's the matter?" only to turn around shaking her head because she knows me, oh, so well.

I wrote my first drama by the end of high school. My best friend's father said that it was the best thing he had read in ten years. Of course, he was a very kind and polite gentleman. I kept my drama in a manila envelope until I lost it seven years later over the Rimac river in Lima, together with everything else I had left, just an old bag full of clothes and papers. I was 19 then.

I wrote my first book three years later, when I was a famous and widely read journalist and columnist in Lima, and I kept it hidden among my papers for another seven years. I saw it published in La Paz, me already married and a well known journalist and columnist in Bolivia. I was 27 then.

My first novel, *Sombra de Exilio,* made me famous but not rich in Bolivia and I spent about three years as the new young literary talent *du jour* until I wrote my second novel, *Anton*, and people wrote long reviews in most of the national papers when it came out. None of them said bad things about me or my book. A few said they had never seen a book like that in their whole life. I tended to see *Anton* as the Bolivian *Ulysses*. Now I believe I was a little spoiled then, perhaps.

I then took advantage of my employment with Braniff, the best airline in the world for its employees, and made a 20-day tour with a bag full of copies of my *Anton* that took me to Montevideo, Buenos Aires, Santiago, Lima, Bogota, Miami, New York City, Chicago, Dallas and back to La Paz, but I could not find an editor for my books. I made many new friends, though.

Back in La Paz and with three kids already, I went to jail for a first time because the military did not like my writing style and spent a week inside a rotten cell. When I came out I wrote *Morder el Silencio* and spent the next seven years trying to publish it. I published it fifteen days before the worst Bolivian military coup ever, the cocaine coup in 1980, and the military burned my book and sent me again to exile to Lima, or so I thought.

It was not to be in Lima but in the U.S. When my plane stopped in Lima and I met some friends from my young days as a reporter, they told me on the tarmac that the military in Peru would send me back to the military in Bolivia, so I went back to my seat in the Lufthansa plane that had smuggled me from La Paz and sat there, silent and worried, until I landed at JFK. I asked for political asylum and I knew that with a bit of luck it would be granted because I had come to the U.S. twenty years before as a young, famous and handsome boy from Peru with the best journalism fellowship in the world. So I bet the CIA knew about me whatever it needed to know, I won, and I was shown a tiny metal door that opened America to me.

I spent another seven years walking up and down Manhattan hoping to find an editor for my *Morder el Silencio*. I could not find any. It took a mysterious lady with a sad smile to perform that miracle, and my *Biting Silence* came out in 1987. I never made a cent from royalties, but my book went around the world. I know because I got emails about *Biting Silence* from Toronto, Seoul, Tokyo and places like that. By then I had bought my Apple IIe and my Mac and a wonderful LaserWriter II. My children were in their last years of high school and we all lived in Bethesda, Maryland, even if we were not wealthy, as everybody there seems to be.

It took a few years more, until 2003, for a second edition of *Biting Silence* to come out into the world. This editor went broke a year or two later and did not pay a cent on royalties either, but by then there was a place called Amazon.com and somebody was making money with my book.

Five years later, I learned to make books starting from a Word file and had written four or five new books. I made them from the writing to the editing, the PDF version, the second PDF version, the cover, an ISBN code bar and most of the intricacies you have to learn to get one, and I could say that I was really—quite literally— the author of these books. Even the mistakes were mine.

I had also learned to use Google and Yahoo to my advantage and now both of them sell books for me. I have my own Web site. I get messages about my books from places like Toronto, Seoul, Tokyo, Bogota, Panama, London, Madrid and Milan. I have made $123.45 from my books since 1970. And somebody is still making money from the first and second editions of *Biting Silence.*

I am 70 now. I had a quadruple bypass in 2000. I have problems with my legs. I have problems with my eyes. I will stop reading any day now. I am functionally deaf. My stomach is not working well these days. I am too fat. I'd better say that I look too fat because I am not that fat. My arms look like chopsticks.

Why am I not as famous as, let's say, Puig, Donoso or Allende? After 65 years of reading and writing I hope I hold the truth about this. It is because of fate, luck, friends, fashion and, perhaps, talent or the lack of it. I have seen a lot of people that write trash and turn it into gold. I am not surprised by this miracle, nor should anybody be. People like reading trash, and getting sentimental to pretend life is a can of soup. Nothing new about that.

No. What stopped me in my way to be famous and make a few dollars with my books is the Million Dollar Wall. I know myself quite well when it comes to fate (it's against me), luck (I don't have it), friends (a few only, without any influence) fashion (I spit on it) and, perhaps, talent or the lack of it (nothing spectacular, but I have what it takes: I have faithful readers in Toronto, Seoul, Tokyo, Bogota, Panama, London, Madrid and Milan, besides La Paz and Lima). If I could live 300 years longer, I would be famous and almost wealthy thanks to my books.

It is just a matter of being "discovered." And you are "discovered" if you have enough time or money, right? I do not have the time. That's only natural. And I do not have the money. I have never had a million dollars to promote and "push" my book as they do with every "best-seller". I cannot be "discovered," therefore, and my long war to reach all kinds of people with my books was never a question of talent or the lack of it. It was, simply and clearly, a question of money, of the Million Dollars Wall that I cannot defeat because I do not have that kind of money. My pension as an old man who used to work for UPI is a monthly $699.98.

So, how fair was this battle of mine in the realm of the System? And who could be proud of such a System? The book industry is a monopoly these days, and all newspapers and magazines promote the same books week after week and never care about talent or the lack of it. It is always because somebody put a million dollars behind each of those books and every journalist wants a few dollars more, right?

It is easy to sell books if somebody spends a million dollars of marketing on a book in the hope of making ten million even if he knows that book is trash. They do that every day and then they sell a thousand copies without losing their jobs.

I could do it any day, even in my days of declining health. So I am very proud of having sold a thousand copies of some books I made with my own hands. Google and Yahoo and Amazon helped me, yes, but there was no money at all to advertise them. It could be that some of my books are good. Well, for a few people at least. But it is horrendous to know that I can die any day now and will not win my struggle to be "discovered" only because God did not give me a million dollars to show the world that I am a writer.

Sometimes I remember John F. Kennedy, the idol of my youth, saying that life is not fair. Life was not fair to him either. It gave him a million or two to become the idol of my youth and now we know what he did. You can imagine what I think today about Kennedy, his sayings and all that jazz.

But, because I am in America, I am betting that this story will translate into a miracle that could smash the Million Dollar Wall. It takes only for you, my potential reader, to "discover" me. Just ask any bookstore, digital or not, about my books and throw twenty bucks away to make me happy.

Thank you very much.

---

http://www.avonvac.com
avonvac@att.net

On *Biting Silence*

Report-1980
Center for Inter-American Relations
Tit1e of Book: <u>Morder el Silencio</u>

Critical evaluation. If possible make specific comparisons or contrasts with other Latin American works that have been translated into English or books written in English.
I think that <u>Morder el Silencio</u> is a fine book. It is an indignant and very moving condemnation of injustice and dictatorship in Latin America (and, by extension, the rest of the world) and, at the same time, an equally moving affirmation of the loyalties and sensibilities that can be maintained even under the regime of The Beast. In the best sense of the word the novel is relevant; it deals with terror sanctioned by law, the impulses of conscience (those acted upon and those ignored), responsibility and engagement——the inescapable social and personal facts of being alive in the 20th century. In its profound observations of political and individual corruption it can be compared to <u>Conversation in the Cathedral</u> –– in its stormy ethical statement, to the works of to Solzhenitsyn. In its somber blend blending of history and imagination to <u>Pedro Páramo</u>. Von Vacano mentions <u>For Whom the Bell Tolls</u> many times and that book may be the ultimate source of his vision: people trapped in historical circumstance, partisanship that absolutely convinces the reader of its fairness and balance, a very deep sense of the difference between viciousness and virtue and, hanging over all, the human doom that can only be changed by the kind of absurd, radical and non—revolutionary posture that makes for martyrs or conservatives who have gone beyond loyalty to either capitalism or communism.

The novel is strong and compelling. I hope it will be widely known and discussed, for it is an important statement about a social and existentially determined tragic sense of life (Von Vacano repeatedly uses the term coined by Unamuno; according to the author Morder el Silencio is a 'nivola" rather than a "novela.") It deserves translation into many languages.

Suitability of book for translation into English. Special difficulties such as regional language.
The book should be translated into English soon. The language is straightforward—fairly colloquial, with references to contemporary political life (e.g. acronyms for gov't. agencies).

300 Word abstract of Sections 1—8.
Morder el Silencio deserves the immediate attention of American publishers and the American reading public; It is well—written, politically and philosophically significant, serious and deeply felt, and not at all sermonizing. It has the immediacy of a book written by someone who is in the midst of living through what he writes about, and the universality of one composed by a man who has come to understand that what allows human beings to terrorize, brutalize. and deceive other human beings is never a purely local phenomenon.

(And then, the Center for Inter-American Relations killed this book. It was the only known case among hundreds, perhaps a thousand books. Why? There was never an explanation.)

..

..